Hinata Bocco

David Nakano

Published by David Nakano, 2024.

This is a work of fiction. Similarities to real people, places, or events are entirely coincidental.

HINATA BOCCO

First edition. June 26, 2024.

ISBN: 979-8227916365

Written by David Nakano.

Table of Contents

Chapter 1

A red bicycle

The song of the cicadas marks the beginning of summer in Tokyo and resonates like a symphony, with each species contributing a unique melody. Some emit monotonous hums, while others unleash varied cries covering a wide range of octaves, creating a melancholic ambiance. For Joseph, an asthmatic child, this chorus of insects would become a metaphor for his own transformation.

At the age of five, Joseph was carried by his grandmother on her back, through the alleyways of Akasaka, wrapped in the soft fabric of her kimono. His interlocked fingers formed an arc around her neck, creating a touching image of comfort. He could hear himself wheezing, like cries for help of the cicadas, a timid and shameful expression of his condition as a sick child, while observing his siblings, Michael and Susanne, enjoying robust health.

She moved with measured steps, her getas (Japanese wooden sandals) making distinct clacks on the pavement as she walked up the narrow alley of Akasaka 9-chome to the wide boulevard of Gaien Higashi Dori. Gently cradling Joseph, she strolled slowly along the broad sidewalk, passing by a clothing store, a florist, and a bookshop. A peculiar clip clopping sound briefly awakened Joseph, allowing him to catch a glimpse of the tall silhouette of a mounted police officer on horseback. The familiar sound of car engines on the big boulevard eventually soothed him again.

Grandmother hoped that these walks would serve as a remedy for Joseph's health, offering him the chance to breathe fresh air away from home. Spring brought its share of pollen, and the neighbors, the Kirishimas, maintained a vast flower garden with hydrangeas, chrysanthemums, roses, tulips, and other exotic plants. Pollen and dust triggered Joseph's asthma attacks. Before heading home, Joseph sometimes woke to the shrill caws of crows perched high above on telephone poles, or to the melancholic bugle of the tofu vendor pulling the cart behind his bicycle. A gentle breeze rustled the maple leaves above the neighbor's wall, and a few cherry blossom petals swirled and fell to the ground.

The Tanaka family settled in a spacious house in the heart of Tokyo, in the Akasaka district. Thomas, the father of Japanese-Hawaiian descent, a Nisei (second generation) of American nationality, left his island of Oahu to work in Tokyo in the post-war period, residing there from 1946 to 1966. He was part of the American M.I.S. (Military Intelligence Service) contingent, commissioned by the U.S. government during post-war reconstruction and surveillance. American military bases were established in various prefectures in Japan, hosting over 50,000 Americans, a quarter of whom were of Asian descent, like the Tanakas. Thomas met Tokiko, a native Japanese woman who worked as a translator for the Americans in the military base office. They married and had three children: Michael, Joseph, and Susanne.

It was Grandmother who accompanied Joseph for a few days at Dr. Sato's residence in the Setagaya ward. The mere mention of "Setagaya" filled him with apprehension, anticipating the inevitable shots, especially the bitter powdered medicine, and the sleepless nights in their upstairs guestroom. He would invariably vomit the medicine, and the kind doctor suggested mixing the powder with sugar and chocolate. Despite this, the bitter taste persisted, making complete ingestion difficult. Suppositories, injections, powdered medicine, were part of Joseph's daily routine. They would spend two or three nights at the doctor's before returning home, only to find themselves back in Setagaya a few weeks later.

During the night, the room was illuminated by a simple paper mâché lantern when Joseph had his asthma attacks. Grandmother would insert a tongue depressor, or a chopstick into his mouth, and Joseph would bite down on it, trembling, struggling to regain his breath. Sinuses were blocked, lungs affected by advanced bronchitis, and he breathed with an open mouth, emitting audible wheezes. Late one evening, with neither chopstick nor a pencil within reach in time, Grandmother placed her thumb in his mouth. From then on, she proudly bore a purple thumbnail, reminding the whole family of her affection and care. Capsules eventually appeared in the pharmacy, and Grandmother took on the daunting task of filling these empty capsules with the white powder. Gradually, Joseph grew accustomed to swallowing these large capsules, and with the right doses of medication, he finally began to heal. The refrain of a traditional song that Grandmother sang while playing the shamisen infused him with hope to continue, "Hana no abura wo choito tsukete" (Rub some oily beads of sweat from your nose onto the hands for luck and happiness).

The American school was located within the United States military base "Washington Heights" in the Yoyogi ward. Students came from various regions of the United States, with a diversity of races including Caucasians, Blacks, and Asian Americans: Japanese, Chinese and some Korean. Most families resided in Washington Heights in the housing units, but a few privileged ones, like the Tanakas, had their residences outside of the base, in various parts of Tokyo.

Joseph inherited his older brother Michael's hand-me-down clothes, as well as some toys and items he no longer needed, including his bicycle. With his gradual recovery from the illness, this reddish-brown bicycle quickly became his favorite pastime. He rode around the alleys behind the house, and eventually, he dared to ride on the broad sidewalk of the boulevard. He discovered the descent to

Hinokicho Park, passing by the ominous komainu (lion dog) statues guarding the entrance to the Nogi-Jinja Shinto shrine. Under the pretext of needing a new pen or pencil, he regularly took this route to go to the stationery store, located 500 meters past the descent. This route became a motivation to study well. However, while engaging in physical activities at school, he quickly realized he would never follow in Michael's athletic footsteps. After a few months, he realized that the reddish color of the bicycle was actually rust, but he continued to ride when he came home from school.

Living in the Minato-ku ward of Tokyo, in the neighborhood of Akasaka, was akin to residing in a prestigious area in Paris, such as Saint-Germain-des-Prés or Trocadéro. It was a special arrangement reserved by the American government for certain Asian-American families and some Caucasian families. The military base established in 1946, Washington Heights, not only included housing for families but also sports facilities, shops, a large supermarket, a cinema, a bowling alley, an Officer's Club, as well as an American school ranging from kindergarten to high school.

The Smith brothers, Clayton and Sandy, owned a pair of non-venomous green snakes as pets, and they often took them for walks, showing them to Michael. It was magical to see these snakes shed their skin, and the brothers kept a few pieces of their dry skin, which they offered as talismans believed to bring wealth. Joseph cherished a piece in his wallet. He tagged along with his brother everywhere, crossing parks, temples, and alleys. When Michael bought tickets at the subway station, a ticket puncher awaited passengers at the turnstile, creating a magical sound with his puncher - ta tin ta tin ta tin tin tin, ta tin tin ta tin tin tin... - pausing only to punch each ticket, finding his rhythm as if playing a musical instrument, the sound resonating to the trains. Getting off the train at Shibuya station, the Smith brothers, hiding their snakes under their clothes, emphasized their reptiles' kindness by pointing to the display window of a specialized store.

Fascinated, they watched large snakes, some venomous, with their triangular heads.

Michael, Joseph's older brother by two years, was 12 when he was selected for the U.S. Armed Forces baseball team, the All Stars, comprising the best players from American schools in Japan. Meanwhile, Joseph stayed home due to his fragile health, dedicating himself to reading and homework. Susanne, Joseph's younger sister by three years, took piano lessons, and one day, a black piano arrived at the house. The entire family eagerly followed Michael's baseball exploits. Every year, a World Championship for Little League was held in the United States, bringing together the best teams from around the world. If the All Stars won matches against Japanese teams, they could advance to the Little League World Series in the U.S. During the crucial match against the Japanese national team, the whole family drove to the baseball park at the American base in Tachikawa.

The game was intense, resulting in a tie 0-0 until the 9th inning. Both teams played exceptionally well and the Japanese pitcher, a giant of 1.85m, proved formidable. An unexpected event, an error, allowed the Japanese team to score and win the match 1-0. Joseph cried for the first time in public, after having watched the game in the bleachers, showing his unwavering support for his brother. Despite the defeat, the family continued to congratulate Michael and his team for their remarkable performance.

Chapter 2

Bicycle with a basket

As the 1964 Tokyo Olympics approached, two years before the event, the entire Washington Heights area was abandoned, and became the famous Olympic Village to host athletes from around the world. The Tanakas were obliged to move, and a dozen Japanese-American families were relocated to new housing on the North Camp Drake military base, while the American school was located at South Camp Drake. The two bases were connected by the presence of American forces in the north and Japanese Self-Defense Forces in the south. Most of the families moved either to Grant Heights in the northwest of the capital or to other American military bases.

In his first year at Narimasu High School, Michael easily integrated into all sports teams, from American football to basketball, wrestling, and track and field. However, running was not Joseph's forte, and he often sought refuge in the library to find the tranquility needed for reading and became adept at using the card catalogue. Meanwhile, to enhance his sports training, Michael asked their parents to find him a new bicycle for rides around Camp Drake.

Michael was often absent due to his athletic commitments, and Joseph obtained permission to use his older brother's bike. He discovered a half basketball court that no one seemed to use. Playing alone with the ball Michael had left behind, he enjoyed scoring imaginary baskets. This solitary pastime became a daily routine for Joseph. In junior high school, despite his doubts about his skills, he tried out for the basketball team. To his great surprise, he was chosen to be part of the team, although smaller than the other players. The practices were tough, but Joseph discovered in basketball the sport that was missing from his life. During games against other schools, Joseph only played a few minutes at the end to give rest to key players of the team. Nevertheless, he shared with his teammates the adventure of traveling by bus for hours to face other teams.

Always in the shadow of his brother, Joseph aspired to being like him, with friends both in sports and at school. Michael had a special friend, Ray, a guitar master handicapped by a bone disorder that gave him a hunched stature and small frame. However, when he played the guitar, whether electric or acoustic, everyone fell silent to listen. Ray became Michael's "sensei"(teacher) and close friend who regarded him as his protegé teaching him various chords and techniques.

Meanwhile, Joseph listened to music on the radio, his favorite artist being the English band, the Beatles. He couldn't quite grasp the blues that his brother practiced at home. To find peace and serenity, Joseph would ride the bicycle to the library to find new books, which he could borrow for a week. This literary refuge became a sanctuary for Joseph, allowing him to escape and nurture his passion for reading.

Discovering so many books in such a rich context as Japan, Joseph found himself confronted with a silent conflict between Japanese life imbued with Shintoism and Buddhism, and the Christian education he received at the American school. This dilemma was often exacerbated during his readings, where he struggled to grasp passages alluding to the Holy Bible. The Tanakas had a small butsudan (Buddhist altar) at home, where incense was burned and offerings of rice cakes or fruit were placed. Paradoxically, every year, the family celebrated Christmas with a beautifully decorated tree and gift exchanges, even though the children had little information about the origin of this Christian holiday. While living in Akasaka, two young Japanese girls suddenly asked Joseph, with cute pronunciation, "what's Sanpakurozu?" referring to Santa Claus. The memory of not being able to give a satisfactory answer to these two girls lingered shamefully every Christmas.

During the Christmas holidays, Joseph reminisces about his childhood. Although the entire family didn't read the Holy Bible, at the age of six in Elementary school, Joseph was selected to play one of the Wise men in a play celebrating the birth of Jesus. He was apprehensive about his role, but with a trembling voice at the beginning, he managed to sing correctly during his performance. This raises the question of whether Joseph was already baptized, given his commitment to Christian lyrics during this portrayal.

Yet, Joseph's first-grade teacher noticed him as a "very timid child." Every day, a student was chosen to share something from their life in the "Show and Tell" segment. Days passed, and Joseph was preoccupied, wondering what to do for his turn, feeling the teacher's compassionate gaze. The big day arrived, and to everyone's surprise, he performed the entire song "Diana" by Paul Anka. This song was part of the collection of 33 rpm records at home, and Joseph listened to it daily on the RCA Hi-Fi console. Miss Izuo, the Japanese-American teacher, was so surprised that she wanted to meet with the parents. Paul Anka performed in Tokyo, and Joseph's parents escorted him to this live concert, happy that their timid son had finally come out of his shell.

In junior high school, new challenges presented themselves to Joseph, especially with subjects like science and algebra, which proved difficult to master. Fortunately, the physical education teacher, Samuel, a tall Hawaiian, saw Joseph's potential outside of these complex subjects. Being Michael's brother, who had left his mark on the track and field records at the school, Joseph was encouraged to join the non-sprinters group, which focused on running longer distances at a more moderate pace.

Before the end of the school year, an inter-school competition was organized at one of the largest American bases, Tachikawa. Middle and high school students took the school bus, a 2-and-a-half-hour journey for a day of athletics. Joseph was nervous from the start of the 800 yard race, but he was relieved to find a fellow student from his school, Gary. At the starting line, his heart was pounding so hard he was afraid of passing out. Encouraged by Gary, who ran alongside him, Joseph kept pace. Gary finished fourth, and Joseph fifth. During the announcements of the day, Michael's name was often mentioned, having won first or second place in sprint races. A race official came to ask to sign a sheet for the results. All runners from first to fifth place had to sign, although the list by school was available. Exhausted from the race, Joseph's signature was not very legible. The announcement of the results was made on the microphone. Alas, with his signature being unreadable, over the loudspeaker, it came out as "Taschenko" from Drake Junior High... a Russian student? This small victory, despite the embarrassment, allowed Joseph to have more confidence in himself.

However, among the academic challenges, one subject stood out for Joseph: the French language and culture course. The teacher, an alluring and delightful American named Kimberly, had lived several years in France and spoke French fluently. The lessons were embellished with photos illustrating French landmarks and images of the Tour de France cycling race. Listening to Kimberly's captivating voice, Joseph dreamed of someday exploring this fascinating country.

Chapter 3

Aloha

In 1966, the Tanaka family leaves Japan due to the father's transfer to a government position in Hawaii, his native island. During the transition, they reside in a rental house in Kaimuki before settling into a new home in Manoa Valley. Each of the children is enrolled in a different school, with Joseph attending Stevenson Intermediate School, Susanne at Manoa Elementary School, and Michael at Roosevelt High School. From the first day, Joseph expresses his disappointment at the lack of French classes and the persistence of algebra-focused mathematics. The father, outraged by the local education system, intervenes with the principal of Roosevelt High School to allow Joseph to take geometry and French classes in the afternoons.

Despite the challenges of geometry, Joseph excels in French, earning the highest grades in the class. On weekends, he loses himself in his paperback books while Michael is out with his friends. Meanwhile, Susanne continues her piano lessons and opts for the oboe in music class, adding an original musical touch to the house.

One Saturday afternoon, the family's Japanese friends, the Katsumotos, come to visit. They propose a tour of the island by car and ask Joseph to accompany his old friend Wayne. However, absorbed in his reading, Joseph declines the invitation, remembering an embarrassing situation at Wayne's house when they were children. Wayne had proudly shown his collection of about fifty miniature cars, while Joseph only had two of Michael's unwanted cars and

Grandmother's abacus, his imaginary truck. Besides, he preferred to stay in the world of the Brothers Karamazov.

Caroline, who resided in one of the houses on the same military base in Camp Drake, exuded an independent aura. She was three years older than Joseph and was often seen with a classmate, Kate. Although Joseph's love remained an unshared secret, his affection for Caroline persisted, occupying his thoughts between readings and bike rides. When the family settles in Hawaii, Joseph is surprised to receive a call from Caroline. She invites him to share a meal with her at the Ala Moana Shopping Center. During the conversation about their memories in Japan, they realize that the admiration was mutual. After their reunion, Caroline takes Joseph by the arm and invites him to her rental home, just four blocks from the mall. It is in this closeness that Joseph experiences his first kiss in the bedroom, marking the end of innocence and the beginning of a new life for the young man.

As Joseph reflects on Caroline upon returning home, he contemplates the existential happiness their recent encounter could bring. His thoughts drift back to his six-year-old self, when he first tasted a Japanese cookie, the Hato Saburé. Despite his illness, the delicate taste of this cookie brought him immeasurable joy, unlike any other snack at home. Convinced that the name was Japanese, with "Hato" meaning dove and the cookie taking the shape of this bird, Joseph, as he learned French, discovers that the word "Saburé" comes from French pastry vocabulary (sablé). Could this experience have been a prelude to his later passion for French language and culture? The crunch of the dove's wings always before the head, would remain a joy similar to Proust's with his madeleine. The Hato Saburé, given as "Omiyage" or gifts during visits, arrived in a yellow metal box adorned with an illustration of a dove. The creator was a Japanese chef in Kamakura who had obtained a large quantity of butter at a time when this ingredient was rare in Japan.

Joseph suffered from frequent nosebleeds. These incidents sometimes occurred in front of his classmates or at home, causing intense embarrassment. With a drop of blood slowly trickling from his nostril, Joseph felt ashamed of the resulting red stain, either hiding in a corner or seeking refuge in the bathroom. He desperately searched for a tissue or used the sleeve of his shirt to wipe away the blood, then hid after inserting pieces of paper or fabric into his nostrils to absorb the flow.

Muneo, a friend of Joseph since Camp Drake and the husband of his aunt Masako, played a special role in these delicate moments. Ten years older, Muneo had recently become a professional boxer, adopting the ring name "Lightning Mac." When he saw Joseph's nosebleed, he took an unusual approach by delivering a sharp blow behind the neck, causing an immediate stop to the bleeding. This method, often used in the ring where boxers are prone to nosebleeds, showed Muneo's resourcefulness in helping Joseph manage these situations.

Joseph longs to reconnect with Caroline, but reality delivers disappointment. Unable to contact her by phone, weeks stretch on without hope. One day, passing by the bookstore at Ala Moana Center, he catches sight of her in a coffee shop, holding hands with an older man. Despite the regret that settles in, Joseph realizes she has found her happiness, adding a new layer of melancholy to his thoughts taking him back to Japan.

The memory of his childhood resurfaces. Kazuhiko, nicknamed Kazu, Michael's close Japanese friend, and next door neighbor, becomes an unwitting hero to Joseph. During a walk in the neighborhood, Joseph mimics the exploits of his brother and Kazu on the debris of a demolished house. However, the adventure goes awry, and Joseph is seriously injured after slipping from a ledge and falling onto broken glass. Kazu, along with Michael, carries him home running and calls for help. At the emergency room of the Sanno Hospital, Joseph receives three stitches above his eye. Once recovered, the two brothers visit Kazu to express their gratitude for his instinctive aid. These moments mark turning points in Joseph's life, punctuated by regrets and unexpected encounters.

Kazu shared his new toy, a tiny portable record player, which fascinated the two brothers. Together, they listened to the American song "Green Fields" by the Brothers Four, appreciating the harmony and poetry of the lyrics. A few days later, in Michael's absence, Joseph dared to return to Kazu's to listen to the captivating song again. However, this time, the incident took a tragic turn.

Enthralled by the music, Joseph only vaguely heard the calls of Yo-chan (Yoshiko), the Tanaka's maid, who was looking for him. In her concern and gesticulations, she was attacked by the guard dog of the house, a German Shepherd, and seriously injured. When Joseph finally arrived there with Kazu, he discovered Yo-chan laying still on the pavement and realized that his presence at Kazu's had indirectly led to the accident. Yo-chan was rushed to the hospital for over a dozen stitches, leaving Joseph with a deep sense of guilt. Despite her recovery, Joseph struggled to face Yo-chan, fearing to speak to her because of the weight of shame and sadness upon him.

The Tanakas enjoyed the privilege of having a domestic helper at home, a welcomed aid for the busy mother of three. At that time, she was extremely occupied, attending American cooking classes several times a week. She also dedicated herself to various Japanese artistic activities, ranging from bonkei (creating miniature Japanese landscapes) to embroidery, ikebana (Japanese flower arrangement), making Japanese dolls, and leathercraft. During family meals in their new home in Honolulu, the father expressed his delight, declaring the meal a success and highlighting the culinary skills that mother had acquired over time. Sipping an after dinner digestif, he fondly recalled, "When I met her, she didn't even know how to boil water."

Chapter 4

Schwinn

At Roosevelt High School, Joseph immerses himself in the world of "cool" students by succumbing to smoking. Encouraged by his brother and classmates who smoke the menthol cigarettes "Kool," he joins the group of smokers who gather in the men's restroom between classes. Working part-time at the Safeway supermarket in Manoa, Joseph also shares cigarette breaks with his colleagues. However, a significant realization occurs thanks to his older Californian friend Greg, who makes him aware of the consequences of smoking on lifespan.

Greg, a tall surfer measuring 1.9m, asserts that every cigarette costs ten minutes of life. Initially skeptical, Joseph disregards this notion until he notices his inability to touch his toes a few weeks later. Greg's words then resonate in his mind, and Joseph decides to end his dependency. Chewing gum, he channels his energy into learning the harmonica, finding a new passion that helps him overcome the urge to smoke. Greg's life, marked by the loss of his father due to lung cancer, serves as a powerful lesson to Joseph about common dangers.

Joseph rediscovers his passion for cycling thanks to two classmates from high school, Timothy and John, who are members of a folk-acoustic group with the future international artist Yvonne. They would ride their bikes to school locking the bikes around a metal post and would notice Joseph watching them often. One day the brothers offer Joseph to buy one of their Schwinn Super Sport, a ten-speed bike, as they would soon be leaving Hawaii, moving to California.

This purchase revives in him the joy of bike rides he had experienced in Japan. With his new bike, Joseph explores the roads and trails around Honolulu, rediscovering a forgotten freedom. Every ride between home and school becomes a revitalizing experience, taking less than fifteen minutes. Carrying his books in a backpack, Joseph feels in harmony with the fresh air, inhaling scents of the plumeria flowers, ripe guavas and mangoes along the roadside. These bike escapades offer him a refreshing perspective and a renewed connection with the beauty of the Hawaiian environment.

At Safeway, Joseph is offered a position in the fresh produce department, but initially, he doesn't have access to the delicate vegetables on the "wet rack". These products, requiring regular watering, such as the varieties of lettuce and cabbage, watercress, celery, spinach and parsley are the responsibility of experienced employees in the department. Working in this prestigious section is considered a promotion in the store, moving Joseph away from the groceries department.

Keith, a stylish and "cool" man in the department, is in charge of the "wet rack". He has a striking Hawaiian girlfriend, Kalani, who sometimes visits him at the store with her friend Madeleine, a charming Chinese-American girl. When Joseph learns that Madeleine is single, he waits for an opportunity. With his bicycle not available after two flat tires, he uses the family car to drive to university the next day. As he desperately searches for parking space, he is surprised to encounter Madeleine halfway to the university. His awkward response to her greeting leaves Joseph regretting his lack of preparation for this unexpected encounter.

Joseph, full of admiration, decides one day to ask Rita, one of the two Indonesian women at the store, out on a date. Five years older than Joseph, Rita and Laura work at the checkout counters or in the office, always with big smiles that would put everyone at ease. In an attempt to impress, Joseph dresses in a suit and tie before picking her up in the car at Rita's residence in Aeia. For this date, Joseph has booked a table at the Bistro on Kapiolani Boulevard, a new restaurant offering French nouvelle cuisine. The dinner goes well despite Rita's language barrier, as she doesn't understand the menu. They have fun, and the meal is a delight for both. On the way back home, Joseph suggests perhaps inviting Laura, her cousin, next time.

The next day at work, Keith, with a mischievous smile, questions Joseph about how the evening went. Joseph responds by explaining that it was just a good friendly dinner. However, Keith humorously reveals that Laura is Rita's partner and that they live together. This revelation leaves Joseph somewhat perplexed.

One day a new Japanese employee, Keizaburo Iketani, joins the Safeway team in Manoa. Initially assigned to the Safeway headquarters on Beretania Street in Honolulu, he is transferred to Manoa due to the presence of Japanese-American staff. Joseph, already a member of the Fresh Produce department, is delighted that his boss Masa considers him a valuable asset to communicate with Iketani-san as Masa and his colleagues' Japanese vocabulary was limited to some "pidgin" or colloquial Japanese-Hawaiian expressions.

Nicknamed Ike by his colleagues, he was initially lost and confused, knowing only a few words in English. Despite his own limited use of his native language in daily life, Joseph starts speaking Japanese with Ike to help him adapt. Over time, Ike becomes a great friend and mentor to Joseph.

During his first days at Safeway, Ike shares a funny story with Joseph. One evening, after work, he walks to his temporary accommodation at the Nakamura Hotel, 6 kilometers from Safeway Manoa. On the way, he stops at a gas station upon seeing a huge machine with the word "ICE." Thinking it's ice cream because he's hungry, Ike inserts coins into the machine but is startled when a huge block of ice falls into the metal bin, producing a thunderous noise.

Chapter 5

Raleigh Record & Pro

At the University of Hawaii, Joseph embraces a diversity of subjects, from philosophy to chemistry, English, Japanese, mathematics, and French. Laden with a huge stack of books for his classes just acquired at the bookstore, he encounters a high school friend, Bob. He was dozing on the freshly cut green lawn under a tree, when Joseph called out to him. Astonished by the burden of books, Bob asks if he's serious. Memories of high school resurface as Joseph proudly shows off his new Raleigh Record bicycle, having sold his former bike to Bob.

However, the university is not without its challenges. One day, emerging from his chemistry class, Joseph discovers that his bicycle has been stolen, a heartbreaking experience. But with determination and earnings from his part time job at Safeway, he invests in a new high end bicycle, reigniting his passion for cycling. With his new Raleigh Professional bike, he joins the Hawaii Bicycle League, mingling with passionate cyclists for training circuits around Kapiolani Park, and other routes stretching to Waimanalo and Kailua.

At Safeway supermarket, Joseph, as a fresh produce worker, enjoyed some privileges associated with his position. His responsibility was to ensure that fruits and vegetables were fresh and available for customers, working with deliveries from various corners of Oahu island. Although he preferred to stay within his domain, he often found himself at the checkout during busy times for the good of the store.

The bike ride to work had become routine, with his bike safely stored inside the building, next to the fresh produce office. During the holidays, working full-time, Joseph discovered that they received significant containers of fruits and vegetables from the mainland United States and at times so much that they could not store all of the arriving merchandise in the produce department cold space. Joseph would call the meat department workers and get permission to store the surplus of apples and oranges in their refrigerated space in the meat storage area which was larger and at a cooler temperature. However, his visits through the corridors filled with huge hanging meat carcasses left a lasting impression on him. The pungent, heavy odor amidst the vinyl sheets led him to give up meat, becoming a vegetarian while still including seafood and dairy in his diet to maintain his health.

Chapter 6

Gitane Jiten-sha

Within the supermarket, Joseph forged a friendship with Bryan, another cycling enthusiast who also lived in Manoa. Together, they pedaled to Hawaii Bicycle League trainings, exploring new routes, including the climb up Monserat Avenue and the loop around the famous Diamond Head crater.

One day, during a visit to The Bike Shop, Jim, a talented mechanic and renowned cyclist on Oahu, broached the subject of cadence with Joseph. He suggested bringing in a track bike for Joseph to improve his cycling skills, and the idea was positively received. The track bike, a Gitane which cost only a fraction of his racing bike, arrived at the shop, but before handing it over to Joseph, Jim installed a "cheater brake" on the front wheel. The bike was equipped with a fixed gear, meaning the rear wheel continued to turn along with the pedals. This forced Joseph to learn to control his speed using his legs, and if necessary, he could use the front brake to stop, adding an extra challenge to his training and develop his skills. With his new Gitane, Joseph pedaled everywhere, even to university classes. The uniqueness of his track bike, with its fixed speed and unattractive setup for thieves, ensured him unparalleled peace of mind also reminding him of "jiten-sha" (bicycle in Japanese).

On a tranquil Sunday morning, Joseph was exploring the roads of Manoa on his track bike on his way to work. Descending a slight slope, he felt the temptation to accelerate. However, he encountered an unexpected obstacle in the form of a young newspaper delivery boy, maneuvering his Sunday newspapers-loaded BMX bike. Already at a brisk speed, anticipating the young man's movement, Joseph expected him to turn left. Unfortunately, the boy made a sudden turn right in front of him, leading to a collision. Joseph was ejected from his bike, watching it bounce on the road. Instinctively protecting his head using his arms, Joseph slid on the asphalt, ending up with red, scraped elbows. Despite the shock, the boy seemed unharmed and expressed concern for Joseph's condition. Joseph quickly reassured the boy, continuing on his way to Safeway. Upon arriving at work, he skillfully concealed the tear in his shirt with his tie and store apron, bandaged both forearms, and completed his eight-hour shift as usual. It wasn't until he returned home that his mother, noticing the torn shirt, and the red bandages, questioned him about the incident. His mother asked the neighboring doctor to have a look and he took Joseph in his car to his office near University avenue. The good doctor gave Joseph several stitches, an injection, and some painkillers and re-dressed his bandages. Joseph was able to quickly recover from this two-wheeled adventure.

Keith and Larry, two seasoned cyclists and Joseph's colleagues at work, invited him to take on the challenge of climbing Mount Tantalus. Although Joseph hesitated at first, his friends reassured him that the pace would be relaxed, with some stops. It was Joseph's first time tackling a 7 kilometer climb, a winding road snaking through the mountain. From the start of the ascent, he was struck by the impressive silence of the mountain, where only the murmur of the Makiki stream reached his ears. As they gained altitude, the tranquility of the mountain revealed its secrets: the piercing cries of birds, the intoxicating aroma of flowers and fruits in the trees. Various types of mangoes, guavas, avocadoes adorned the treetops and giant ferns provided shade in the lush valleys. 500 meters from the summit, an open-door house caught their attention. Suddenly, a large German shepherd, the property's guard dog, chased after them barking. Joseph narrowly escaped being bitten, sprinting with all his might.

At the summit, they took a break allowing them to admire the breathtaking panorama of Honolulu, with its buildings seeming to shrink and the endless expanse of the Pacific Ocean stretching as far as the eye could see. The climb, despite its challenges, had rewarded Joseph and his friends with a stunning view and unforgettable memories.

Chapter 7

Annyeong Haseyo

Mi-Cha and Seo-Yeon, two young Korean women, were shopping at Safeway with their mother. Joseph noticed them, particularly the second sister who wore dark glasses and held a white cane, revealing her visual impairment. However, the young woman displayed a brave smile as she spoke to her sister, demonstrating her determination despite the obstacles. As they were in the aisle, a pyramid of Hawaiian Sun juice cans on promotion caught their attention at the entrance to the fresh produce section. Seo-Yeon, with her cane, tried to navigate but unfortunately her cane nudged the corner of the pyramid, causing the cans to cascade down. Startled by the noise, she lost her balance, but Joseph, who was nearby, caught her in his arms, preventing a more serious incident. Even though Joseph didn't understand the Korean language, he could feel the emotion in Seo-Yeon's voice, who, after a few tears, called out to her sister in Korean. The two sisters, along with their mother, warmly thanked Joseph for his immediate intervention.

During their next encounter, Mi-Cha and Seo-Yeon apologized for the incident by bowing their heads in a gesture of politeness and introduced themselves to Joseph. The sisters were wearing short Hawaiian summer dresses, and Joseph noticed their fair complexion. He learned that they had come from Seoul to pursue their studies at the University of Hawaii. Joseph mentioned that he was also a student at the university. They bowed their heads again, thanking Joseph for taking the time to talk with them. Mi-Cha, interested in fruits, asked Joseph to choose a watermelon. He taught her how to tap lightly on the melon to determine the sound associated with its quality, a trick he had learned from Masa. As he placed the selected watermelon in their basket, Joseph addressed Seo-Yeon, telling her that from now on, she could choose the next watermelon herself, eliciting a shy smile. This interaction marked the beginning of an unexpected friendship, where despite language barriers, smiles and laughter transcended cultural differences.

A few weeks later, the sisters surprised Joseph by inviting him to their home to celebrate their mother's birthday. With their father on a business trip to Seoul, Joseph found himself as the sole guest for this special occasion. Not having informed them that he was vegetarian, Joseph felt embarrassed that he could not taste all the delicious dishes they had prepared, but the sisters understood the situation perfectly. He had brought a large basket of assorted fruits, decorated with some flowers, as a gift for the celebration. The house, located on the East side of Manoa Valley, in Woodlawn, offered a peaceful view. During dinner, Joseph learned that Mi-Cha was studying law and that Seo-Yeon was devoted to music. The table was filled with fifteen varied dishes, including Kim Chi, seasoned rice, beans, bibimbap, spiced vegetables as well as various fish and meat dishes. After the feast, they relaxed with Korean tea in the living room. Joseph shared information on a sports complex near Manoa Elementary School, with tennis courts and a pool open to all residents of the neighborhood. They decided to meet at the pool, where Seo-Yeon, with her darkened swimming goggles, swam gracefully in perfect synchronization with her sister Mi-Cha, who wore clear goggles. The warm evening and the discovery of their respective passions had strengthened the budding bonds of this unexpected friendship.

Between classes at the university, Joseph sees Seo-Yeon walking with her violin on her shoulder towards Orvis Auditorium. He calls out to her, and she stops, waiting for him to approach. Joseph complimented her courage to walk alone and asked if there was an audition or if she was going to a music class. With a smile, she explained that it was time to practice in the individual rehearsal rooms and invited him to accompany her. In one of these soundproofed rooms, Seo-Yeon took her violin out of its case and began to play a Mozart sonata. From the first notes, Joseph was deeply moved, unable to hold back a few tears. Sensing Joseph's reaction, Seo-Yeon abruptly stopped and asked if everything was all right. Joseph assured her that it was beautiful and encouraged her to continue. However, she reached for Joseph's hand and found his face, feeling his tears on her slender fingers. In Korean, she said "Komapsumnida," or thank you, and Joseph repeated these words with the correct pronunciation. Time seemed to stand still, leading to a first kiss, sealing a moment filled with a sentimental connection.

Chapter 8

Travelers

Before the 1972 school holidays, Joseph, then in his second year at the University of Hawaii, became interested in travel. On the hallway bulletin board at Moore Hall, where he attended French classes, a poster advertised round-trip tickets from Honolulu to London. With an incredible promotional price, the return trip was limited to a two-month stay. Joseph requested leave from his job at the supermarket for the summer and invited friends to join him. Lawrence, a student passionate about painting and art history, and Jim, a philosophy enthusiast and avid reader, accepted the invitation. Both were two years older than Joseph and also friends of Michael.

Upon arrival at Heathrow Airport, they were greeted by Marlene, Lawrence's older sister, who drove them to her "flat" or apartment in London. She worked as a secretary in an import-export company. During their three weeks in the British capital, they discovered the London "Underground" or subway system. They visited the Tate Gallery, the British Museum, and had the exceptional opportunity to see the Tutankhamun exhibition. They also attended Shakespearean plays, including "A Midsummer Night's Dream" at the Regent's Park Open Air Theatre.

With the purchase of a used car, a Volkswagen station wagon, they could soon embark on a journey through several countries. Lawrence, the driver took them to Cambridge to attend a concert by the Kinks, an unforgettable experience. The trip would continue, punctuated by artistic, musical, and cultural discoveries that promised to leave lasting impressions on their memories.

After leaving London, they headed south and arrived in Dover in the late afternoon. The hovercraft, crossing from Dover to Calais, allowed them to board their car onto the ship. Upon arriving in France, Joseph became their official guide, as his friends were not proficient in the language. After finding a simple hotel in Paris, they dedicated an entire day to exploring the Louvre, immersing themselves in art and works spanning through the ages.

Lawrence insisted on visiting the Jeu de Paume and the Orangerie, where paintings by Gauguin, Van Gogh, Degas, and Renoir captivated them, while Monet's Water Lilies in the basement created an unforgettable panoramic magic. Traveling around the city by metro, they discovered iconic landmarks such as the Eiffel Tower and Notre-Dame de Paris. The Sainte-Chapelle, with its breathtaking stained glass windows, particularly left an impression on Joseph, prompting deep reflection on his spiritual journey as a future Christian.

With Lawrence as their art guide, they would visit the Rodin Museum, where they discovered the marble sculptures gleaming in the garden and inside the building. Upon Joseph's suggestion, they took a tour to the Palace of Versailles, strolling through the beautifully manicured gardens dating back to the time of Louis XIV, and visiting the famous Hall of Mirrors with its immense tapestries. Upon exiting, they were awestruck by the gushing fountains, an experience made even more special due to the "Journée des Grandes Eaux" or Fountains Day.

Joseph had developed a habit of buying French newspapers such as France Soir or Le Figaro, not only for the news but especially to follow the Tour de France. Each day, he would discover the summaries of the stages and the exploits of Eddy Merckx, a true cycling legend.

Their journey led them to Lyon, where they spent a night, savoring Lyonnaise cuisine in a small restaurant. The next day, they crossed the border near Geneva, continuing their journey through Zurich before reaching the Italian border. In Pisa, they made a stop to admire the famous leaning tower. In Rome, they marveled at Michelangelo's works in the Sistine Chapel, enthralled by the marble sculpture of the Pietà. Two nights in Florence allowed them to explore the masterpieces of Michelangelo, Botticelli, Titian, Donatello, as well as the rich collections of the Uffizi Gallery, highlighting the artistic legacy of the Medici.

They spent a peaceful night in the small town of Assisi, renowned for its Capuchin monks, whose brown habits allegedly inspired the name of the famous drink, the cappuccino. However, an unexpected incident awaited them upon departure from the inn. As they were about to embark on their journey again, Joseph realized he had forgotten his backpack. A man, alerted by the scene, began gesturing and shouting "baggagio, baggagio." Lawrence stopped the car, and Joseph understood his mistake.

The discovery of Venice proved to be a magical experience for Joseph and his friends, steeped in history and art. Leaving the car behind, they boarded a shuttle boat to reach this unique city, woven with bridges and canals. For four days, they explored the picturesque alleyways, crossed iconic bridges, and discovered artistic treasures hidden in Venetian museums, guided by Lawrence, the art enthusiast. The galleries revealed masterpieces by Venetian masters such as Bellini, Giorgione, Veronese, Titian, and Tintoretto, immersing the travelers in a distant era. Lawrence also introduced them to more contemporary artists like Turner. Near the famous St. Mark's Square, they discovered a modest café in a small square. Under the parasol, amidst the summer heat, they ordered refreshing drinks. At the end of their break, they rose to head back to their small hotel, but an Italian waiter caught their attention – "Signore, Signore!" Joseph had forgotten his camera, left behind on the back of a chair.

Leaving the enchanting canals of Venice was tinged with sadness, but the journey through France, Belgium, the Netherlands, and the experience in Edam added new dimensions to the adventure. Passing through France again, fatigue enveloped them in the car as Lawrence continued to drive, and they found small inns to allow the driver to rest.

Their stop in Bruges, a peaceful city in Belgium, offered a quiet night. Continuing their journey, they crossed into Holland, making a stop in Edam, famous for its cheese. The warm welcome from the owner of a local farm led them to discover the cheese-making process. The enticing aroma and tasting of the soft cheese remained memorable. They concluded their day with local beer, Heineken, purchased at a tiny village store, adding an authentic touch to their Dutch experience.

Amsterdam, while reminiscent of Venice with its canals, presented a different ambiance in the Netherlands. Under Lawrence's guidance, they explored the Rijksmuseum, where masterpieces by artists such as Rembrandt and Vermeer captivated their imagination. The awe-inspiring display of detailed and monumental works from the 17th century prompted Joseph to reflect on his studies in French literature, evoking authors such as Molière, Racine, and Descartes from that era.

Their stay in Amsterdam was also marked by the vibrant colors of the flower market, with an impressive variety of tulips, carnations, hydrangeas, and orchids. Observing Dutch women and men cycling with baskets of vegetables or beautiful bouquets of flowers, Joseph discovered a lively local life. As they departed for France, they returned to Calais to take the hovercraft back to England, thus concluding their journey across Europe with memories rich in art, culture, and adventures.

Chapter 9

Ruv

The return to Honolulu marked the beginning of a new phase for Joseph. Rediscovering his island environment, he decides to take a bike ride from Manoa to Waikiki, along the famous Kalakaua Avenue. The prospect of reconnecting with Korean sisters Mi-Cha and Seo-Yeon leads him to a lagoon-side restaurant. He thinks about the chapters he read by Hemingway and his fondness for Gin and Tonic. Contemplating the Pacific Ocean, Joseph reflects on memories of the recent European journey with his friends. As the drinks flow, he realizes that a dozen, like the writer, would be a perilous undertaking. On the way back to Manoa, he rides at a leisurely pace, crossing the university campus with a familiar sense of security. The tranquil road is scattered with red hibiscus and yellow plumeria. As Joseph pedals slowly a sudden breeze causes a mango to fall near Joseph's bicycle. Upon arriving at Safeway, he feels a certain guilt for leaving his colleagues during the summer months. However, the warm reception from the store manager and colleagues heralds his return to work, thus sealing a well-received comeback. Amid conversations about European sunshine and the effect of alcohol on the Japanese, Joseph feels reintegrated into Safeway's family environment.

The encounter with Mi-Cha and Seo-Yeon at the bookstore marks a joyful reunion. Conversation in Korean evoke a special bond, strengthened by their invitation to the Pizza Hut across University Avenue. Seo-Yeon openly expresses the longing she felt during the summer, and the sisters are delighted to hear some details of Joseph's

European adventures. Living near the university makes daily life easier for Seo-Yeon, a member of the orchestra, and Mi-Cha embarks on a promising internship at a law firm. The parents' pride shined through, reflecting their commitment to their daughters' education and fulfillment. The diversity of paths chosen by the two sisters reflects the richness of their aspirations and talents.

Joseph met with Seo-Yeon at the East West Center's Self-Service cafeteria. After a pleasant lunch, they found themselves caught in a downpour that had just refreshed the air and dampened the campus sidewalks. Concerned for his friend's safety, Joseph offered to accompany her to her music class at the Orvis Auditorium. This warm gesture translated into a protective act as Joseph offered his arm to Seo-Yeon, allowing her to move confidently despite the weather conditions. It was a selfless act that spoke volumes about the sincere friendship between them. As they exited the auditorium, Joseph had waited for Seo-Yeon due to the still damp pavement, and then offered to escort her home to ensure her safety.

The quaint rental house on Hunnewell street was located in a tranquil neighborhood, the street bordered by acacia, mango, avocado and banyan trees. It usually took only ten minutes for Seo Yeon to walk home from the entrance of the University campus. She served Korean tea with a plate of cookies and two types of grapes. Joseph discovered childhood photos of the two sisters, the image of the young girl without dark glasses piquing his curiosity about the cause of Seo-Yeon's blindness. The explanation of the skiing accident, shared with emotion, highlighted the bond between the two sisters and the strength they showed in the face of adversity.

The warm atmosphere continued with the discovery of her classical music collection, Mi-Cha's law books, and books in braille. Thanking her for her hospitality, Joseph stood up, but Seo-Yeon took his hand and led him to her room. Expressing his concern for not having protection, she reassured him with a smile, whispering that she had suffered another consequence of her accident, allowing them precious time together. Hesitant at first, he traced his fingers along the tiny moles of her left cheek and below her lips. She unfastened the ribbon holding her ponytail as Joseph's hands felt her silky black hair fall below her shoulders and he held her tightly.

Chapter 10

Rue de Vaugirard

Joseph continued his studies diligently, particularly excelling in French, and was selected as a candidate for a scholarship offered by the Alliance Française of Hawaii. Coincidentally, another student, Louise, who had been in his classes at the American school in Tokyo, also decided to study in France with a similar scholarship, choosing Montpellier as her destination. Joseph opted for Paris, where he enrolled in courses in French language, civilization and literature at the Sorbonne.

His new residence would be at a dormitory in the 6th arrondissement, 104 Rue de Vaugirard, at La Réunion des Étudiants, a Catholic establishment accommodating up to 200 students, with a dozen places reserved for foreigners. Joseph shared his room with Rino, a student of Italian origin with Canadian nationality. The residence housed students from various backgrounds, like Gary from New York, Fred from Philadelphia, and Anton from Wisconsin. As the sole representative from Hawaii, Joseph was nicknamed "Five-0," a reference to the famous Hawaiian TV series. The warm atmosphere of the residence included a large kitchen with a huge dining area, offering breakfasts with crispy baguettes, croissants, butter, jam, with a choice of coffee, cocoa, or tea along with hot milk in a self-service style. Lunch was served in the same manner but for dinner the Menu of the day, was served with the help of some of the students. Before each meal, Joseph learned to make the sign of the cross in this Catholic setting.

It was the beginning of an exceptional school year in autumn of 1973. He fully immersed himself in the discovery of Paris, initially exploring the surrounding areas as a cool breeze rustled the brown leaves of the maple trees lining the boulevard Montparnasse. Returning from classes, he stumbled upon a hardback French-English dictionary on a bridge over the Seine River at a "bouquiniste" or bookseller. Joseph took advantage of the discounted price, and it was much more comprehensive in complex terms than the small paperback dictionaries. Among his essentials, he always carried with him the Michelin Guide and the metro map to navigate the City of Light.

During his wanderings, Joseph met Anton, his neighbor, who caught him leafing through the Michelin Guide. Anton an art student, offered to show him places not listed in the guide, fascinating places he wished to explore together. With a deep knowledge of art history, Anton aspired to become a museum curator or an art professor. He thus became Joseph's personal guide, taking him to discover monuments, painting and sculpture museums, cathedrals, pointing out Art Nouveau works, surrealist movements, impressionist, classical, and modern art, as well as small and large castles for an in-depth appreciation of French art.

Exploring Paris by bicycle with Anton added a new dimension to Joseph's experience. Borrowing bicycles from Anton's friends, they embarked on a delightful ride to reach the Château Vaux le Vicomte, located 50 km southeast of Paris. This castle, a model for other royal residences, fascinated them with its remarkable architecture and its history linked to the creation of the Palace of Versailles.

Within the vast geometric garden, they enjoyed snacks and refreshments, they brought in their backpacks, relishing the fresh autumn air. Inside the castle, classical paintings, grand tapestries, impressive ceilings, and marble and bronze sculptures captivated Joseph, who listened attentively to Anton's exciting tales about each artwork.

The return to Paris, though marked by an incident with Anton's bike pedal, concluded with a memorable ride along the Champs-Élysées, offering a breathtaking view of the Arc de Triomphe. Back at the Réunion des Étudiants on Rue de Vaugirard, they were in time to shower before joining the dining hall for dinner. A fulfilling day, blending cultural exploration and two-wheeled adventure, further strengthened their friendship.

Chapter 11

Letters

The geographical distance between Paris and Honolulu only heightened Joseph's concern about news from Seo-Yeon. The letters, elegantly written by her sister Mi-Cha, took several weeks to arrive. Each correspondence was eagerly anticipated with palpable impatience. Meanwhile, Seo-Yeon devoted herself intensely to the violin, seeking in music an escape from the separation that had deeply marked their first love.

He learned of the upcoming university orchestra concert, a charity event for disabled children in Hawaii, at the Honolulu International Centre. Seo-Yeon would be in the front row as the solo violinist, which brought Joseph a mixture of happiness and sadness. Although the distance prevented him from being there in person, he didn't want to miss the chance to express his support to her. He found a florist displaying the famous FTD logo (the running man with wings on his feet carrying a bouquet of flowers ; inspired by Hermès, the messenger of Zeus). Joseph arranged for a bouquet of roses to be sent in time for the concert, adding a personal note to express his feelings to Seo-Yeon. He wrote on the card "To Seo-Yeon, Music transcends the vast ocean as my thoughts are with you".

Walking on the bridges of the grand capital, passing by the bouquinistes, he decided to visit the Sainte Chapelle. The magic of the stained glass windows, celebrating biblical events, deeply moved Joseph. Despite a tinge of melancholy thinking about the inability to share this luminosity with Seo-Yeon, he understood that their encounter and the vivid memories of their friendship and love would remain engraved in their hearts.

A few weeks after exams, Joseph is delighted to receive a letter from Honolulu. Seo-Yeon was warmly applauded during the concert, receiving several bouquets, including the largest one from Paris, which deeply moved her. An article published in the Honolulu Star Bulletin, featuring a photo of Seo-Yeon, has made her a prodigy and celebrity in Hawaii. Despite several invitations to the privileged community's parties after the concert, she declined them all, thinking of Joseph. Seo-Yeon continues to progress in her musical career, considering an apprenticeship in violin in the hopes of joining a symphony orchestra, on the American continent or in South Korea. Mi-Cha, delighted and proud of her sister, watches over her well-being. The two sisters eagerly await news from Joseph, emphasizing that no one else in their daily lives has Joseph's kindness and tenderness, and they miss him terribly.

Chapter 12

Hitch Hiker

During the school holidays, Joseph embarks on the adventure of hitchhiking, an experience that starts with a few hiccups. Taking the train to the Versailles station seems like a practical idea, thinking it would be easier to find the right path out of the historic town than directly from the metropolis. However, his first steps out of Versailles turn into a endless meandering through streets and paths. After hours of fruitless walking, he realizes that night is approaching and decides to turn back to find the SNCF station in Versailles.

On the next train bound for Paris Gare de Lyon, Joseph finds himself spending the night in a corner of the station, reminiscent of Beckett's characters, Vladimir and Estragon. Sleep is interrupted by frequent awakenings, fearing potential questioning from the gendarmes (French police). In the morning, he is drawn to the delights of the station café and replenishes himself with fresh croissants and café au lait. Resuming his journey, he finally spots signs indicating directions to Lyon and Marseille, and with the international hitchhiking sign, Joseph joins other travelers waiting for their chance. Luckily, a generous driver picks him up and takes him to Lyon, although fatigue catches up with him during the journey. In Lyon, he discovers a small grocery store, where he dares to try a takeout dish with rice, even if the addition of olive oil holds an unexpected taste for him.

Hitchhiking was an adventure for Joseph, each journey a discovery of unfamiliar places, landscapes, and French landmarks and roads, as described in his readings or depicted on postcards. Though often alone, he embraced the challenges of solitude by immersing himself in the exploration of each new region.

One day, he hopped into a red car driven by a young mother accompanied by her 3-year-old son. Intrigued by the presence of a Japanese hitchhiker, she struck up a conversation and asked various questions. However, her main concern was finding a bakery to buy bread for dinner. Though the ride was short, covering about fifteen kilometers, Joseph grasped the cultural significance of bread in French households, reminiscent of his childhood in Japan where rice is a staple of every meal.

Crossing the border in Saint-Sébastien, Joseph faced a major challenge: the language barrier. While he had managed to converse in French with understanding drivers in France, communicating in Spanish in Spain proved more difficult and sometimes frustrating due to his limited vocabulary. A female driver asked him questions about his faith in God, insisting with the word "Dios". To ensure he wasn't left on the roadside, Joseph repeatedly responded with a simple "si, si".

At times, he found himself alone on the highway for hours without anyone stopping. Walking with his red backpack, he crossed vast orange plantations. Hungry and finding no stores nearby, Joseph allowed himself to pick a few oranges, succumbing to temptation despite being aware of the unlawfulness of his act. His next ride took him in a comfortable sedan, where the driver, a businessman, questioned him about the life of an Asian student in Europe. The car was so comfortable that Joseph quickly fell asleep, the compassionate driver letting him rest. Awakened outside a rustic restaurant, Joseph was invited to lunch and enjoyed a delicious squid with fresh Basque-style spinach.

The following day, Joseph met a charming German family on vacation with their own car. They spoke English, which greatly facilitated communication, and Joseph discovered that the father was a professional photographer while the mother was a model. Together, with their 5-year-old son, they were enjoying the school holidays by exploring new horizons. Whenever the driver spotted a captivating landscape, he would slow down the car and step out to capture photos, thus sharing his passion with Joseph. During this journey, Joseph had the opportunity to use his own camera to immortalize these memorable moments. A village they passed through caught their attention, seemingly split in two by the aftermath of a storm, creating a scene reminiscent of Salvador Dalí's surrealist works. Through the lens of his camera, Joseph captured these enigmatic moments, enriching his collection of visual memories as he hitchhiked through Spain.

In Madrid, Joseph felt a slight regret for not having Anton by his side to explore the Prado Museum. Nevertheless, he immersed himself in the exceptional art on display, discovering the iconic works of masters such as Goya, El Greco, Velasquez, Caravaggio, Bosch, Rubens, and many others. Spending several hours wandering through this immense collection, he delved into the various periods of artistic history.

Finding himself in the streets of Madrid, Joseph realized the discomfort of only knowing a few words in Spanish. However, he recalled the day of solitary walking in Paris before the start of his journey, realizing that each new challenge was an opportunity to overcome linguistic and cultural barriers.

Joseph continued his journey to Algéciras, taking a ferry to Tangier in Morocco. From there, he takes the train to Casablanca, where he would spend a night in a small hostel. Joseph is struck by the warm landscape and the marked cultural differences characterized by the traditional attire of Muslims, Arabs, and pieds-noirs as well as the bustling outdoor markets teeming with brightly colored vegetables, fruits, dried fruits, beans and grains. As he wanders through the souks, Joseph observed pieces of meat displayed in the sun, understanding that customers will soon buy them. Getting acquainted with daily life in Morocco, Joseph explores Marrakech and enjoys fresh mint tea. He takes advantage of the opportunity to speak French in this country, thus adding a new cultural dimension to his adventure.

On the return journey through Spain despite the language barrier, Joseph still appreciates the landscapes along the way, contemplating ruins, aqueducts, and ancient cathedrals, each bearing witness to a bygone era. He is awestruck by the grandiose preparation and colorful decorations for Easter in Seville. Following Anton's advice, he detours to Barcelona and take the bus to Figueras to visit the Dali Museum, where he would discover the original and incredible surrealist paintings by the master.

Crossing the border and returning to France brings great relief to Joseph. In Bordeaux, he meets Roger, a Canadian history professor on a European tour. Although the next planned stop is Paris, Roger is adamant about seeing Mont Saint-Michel. They stop for a night in La Rochelle, where the driver sleeps in the car and Joseph finds refuge in an "auberge"(inn). Although Joseph has already visited Mont Saint-Michel with the group of American students, he is delighted to revisit this unique and historic place. Upon returning to his Parisian abode on Rue de Vaugirard, Joseph discovers a letter from the Korean sisters.

Chapter 13

Parisian Style

Their reunion at the dormitory is marked by the enthusiastic sharing of the adventures experienced during the holidays, discovering common interests. Anton suggests a small excursion through the capital, during which they admire the "Libellule" (dragonfly) entrance of the Porte Dauphine subway station by Hector Guimard. Anton points out the unique baroque façade of the Saint Sulpice church. A visit to the flea market at Porte de Clignancourt reveals a lamp signed by Gallé, a master of the Art Nouveau movement, which Anton considers, despite its high price. He advises Joseph to be wary of counterfeits. Exchanging anecdotes, they discover that they both were in Morocco at the same time, but Anton had met a girl who admired him. Joseph, flashes an enigmatic smile during a refreshing break at a café in the Latin Quarter, hinting to Anton that he might have a well-kept secret.

The French language classes, held three times a week at the girls' hostel at 116 Boulevard Raspail, brought together a diverse group of students, like Joseph and his classmates, hostel residents, as well as some privileged students arriving by car or others walking from the Montparnasse subway station. Emphasis was placed on grammar, and mastering the French language, including lessons on the pronunciation of the dreaded "r" sounds and strict adherence to the rules of politeness, with a categorical prohibition of informal language. An incident involving young Charles, a Chinese student, who had used the informal "tu" in response to a question, had incurred the wrath of the teacher,

Madame Le Fevre, resulting in his absence from class the following days.

As for the literature classes, they took place in a classroom at the Sorbonne, located in the 5th arrondissement. Under the guidance of Monsieur Cordier, a round and corpulent man, students practiced reading and correct pronunciation, often facing impromptu dictations. The featured book on the syllabus was "Un Balcon en Forêt" by Julien Gracq. In a lecture hall, the students delved into civilization lessons, exploring the rich history of this captivating country.

Twice a month, the students enrolled in the same program as Joseph, enjoyed day trips to explore the surroundings beyond the metropolis. These outings included visits to the Palace of Versailles, Vaux le Vicomte, the Loire Valley castles, Mont Saint Michel, Rambouillet, Orléans, as well as the vast vineyards of Épernay, with an unforgettable tour of the Taittinger cellars and a champagne tasting to conclude. Joseph, delighted by the program's offerings, was already looking forward to continuing his studies in French literature. These enriching experiences provided him with a deep understanding of French culture and history.

Every three months, the Dormitory organized a book day where students could acquire books left by other students. The proceeds from this day were then used to support the establishment. On this occasion, Joseph found a pocket-size French Bible, as well as some 19th and 20th-century novels. He was amazed to see the diversity of topics covered, ranging from sciences to mathematics, law, medicine, and politics, with an abundance of books laid out on tables in the central courtyard.

Each month, widows living in the city were invited to share a dinner with the students, usually on Friday evenings as some students took the weekend off to return to their families. This provided enough seating for the dignified ladies. This tradition aimed to provide a moment of conviviality between the young students and the older ladies of the community. A French student recited a prayer to start the dinner, followed by a gourmet meal prepared by the Executive chef of the establishment. Two priests, including Father O'Reilly, also joined the group to pay tribute to the deceased husbands and share these moments of respect and commemoration.

Chapter 14

Return, Love, Regrets

To celebrate their reunion, Joseph invites the sisters to dinner at the Bistro on Kapiolani Boulevard, a restaurant offering a typically French menu, reminiscent of the flavors he discovered in France. Although most of their meals were at the dormitory cafeteria, Joseph takes pleasure in sharing a French gastronomic experience with his friends. The sisters share their progress since his departure. Seo-Yeon has furthered her musical development, receiving apprenticeship offers on the American continent, while Mi-cha has secured a secretary position at a law firm in Downtown Honolulu.

Joseph shares with them his memories of the artworks, architectural landmarks, and museums he discovered in France. As he drives them home, the sisters invite him in for a digestif. While they contemplate their childhood photos together, Joseph expresses his sadness while congratulating the sisters for their resilience in the face of adversity. After sharing a bottle of Médoc at the restaurant, the alcohol's effect causes Joseph to blush. As he gets up to leave, the sisters encourage him to spend the night at their place. He learns that Mi-cha has made a pact to stay by her sister's side, sharing her room to watch over her.

Back at his job at Safeway, Joseph commits to working 40 hours per week. On his days off, he dedicates time to reconnecting with the two sisters. The Manoa pool becomes a peaceful and invigorating spot for them, although Mi-Cha is often absent, busy with her work at the downtown Honolulu office. When the three friends manage to find simultaneous free time, they share lunches at restaurants or venture by car to the east coast, particularly to Makapu, enjoying a picnic at Sandy Beach.

A few weeks after learning the sad news, the two sisters shared with Joseph that their mother was showing the first symptoms of dementia. Faced with this reality, their father was obliged to make the decision to take their mother back to Seoul, to be with family. They still owned a house in the city, in the southern Banpo-dong area, maintained by their mother's sister. This news is a great disappointment for the two sisters, who have become accustomed to tropical life in Oahu, but they are determined to support their mother through this difficult time.

Joseph, saddened by the news and the imminent departure of Seo-Yeon and Mi-cha, wanted to offer a memorable day as a guide-driver, touring the island of Oahu by car. Leaving Manoa, he passed through Makiki and took the winding road up to Tantalus, explaining that he had already traveled this route several times by bike. They were surprised by the challenges their friend had faced, and at the summit, they took photos with the panorama of Honolulu in the background. On the way down, they stopped at another lookout point offering a captivating view of the entire Manoa Valley, and Mi-cha described the details to Seo-Yeon in Korean at each stop. Joseph couldn't hold back his tears, thinking of the darkness that must accompany Seo-Yeon even in these luminous moments of their friendship.

The next stop was the Bishop Museum to explore Hawaii's unique history. Continuing their journey, Joseph drives up Kunia Road, ascending to the plateau past the vast pineapple plantations, with the silhouette of the North Shore on the horizon. The Dole Pineapple concession offered them delicious fresh pineapple juice, and Joseph ordered a coffee to stay alert on the road. Descending the long road to Haleiwa, he explained that the watermelons and vegetables at Safeway came from the agricultural fields in this region.

In the tranquil village of Haleiwa, Joseph treated them to some shaved ice with syrup, a Hawaiian delight at Matsumoto Shave Ice, established in 1951. The picturesque shops delighted the sisters as they looked for souvenirs for their loved ones, perpetuating the cultural tradition of bringing back "Omiyagé" or gifts from a trip. Joseph waited for them while enjoying a cup of coffee. Passing by Haleiwa's famous surfer's spot, the waves weren't huge yet, but one could feel the dramatic power of the ocean hearing the waves pounding and rumbling against the rocks. In Kahuku, they took a lunch break, enjoying local crabs caught the day before in the surrounding waters. Joseph saw their joy as they quickly spoke in Korean, but they apologized for their manners and switched back to English.

As Joseph drove, he reminisced about his first bike race, the Haleiwa Sea Spree he did back in 1972, a two stage race totaling 115 miles. The sisters were amazed that their friend could embark on such an adventure. It was a few months before their first encounter at Safeway, and he was only nineteen at the time. He shared some anecdotes from his childhood marked by illness and recovery. He expressed his hope that a miracle might happen one day for Seo-Yeon to regain her sight, and this remark brought tears to both of them. The journey took them to the town of Laie on the north-east coast, and they spent a few hours at the Polynesian Cultural Center. Hearing the instruments, guitars, ukuleles, and drums, Seo-Yeon was filled with joy. They discovered the different cultures of Tahiti, Hawaii, Fiji, Tonga, Samoa, Cook Islands, each region bringing unique songs and dances.

In Kaneohe, Joseph takes them to the Valley of the Temples, a memorial park and cemetery where hundreds of Hawaiians of various religions, including Buddhism, Shintoism, Protestantism, and Catholicism, are buried. The serenity and lush beauty of this revered space at the foot of the Koolau Mountains is stunning. Mi-cha read some panels in English with historical details to help her sister understand. In the valley background, a light rain revealed a rainbow in front of several waterfalls, giving the area an enchanting and spiritual atmosphere. The Byodo-in Temple, meaning the Temple of Equality, is located in the gardens, a replica of the Uji Temple in Japan. This temple commemorates the centenary of the first Japanese immigrants to Hawaii. Before entering, each one of them rang the sacred bell with the help of a large wooden log, a custom that brings happiness and longevity.

In Kailua, they visit the beautiful Lanikai Beach, and Joseph suggests a quick tour of the town to find Kailua Health Food Store for fresh fruit juices. Joseph decides to take the Pali Highway back instead of going through Makapu to take a shortcut, and visit the Nuuanu Pali lookout. At the Kaneohe junction, the road sign indicates the distance to Honolulu: 8 miles, or 13 kilometers. Upon returning to their home in Manoa, they invite Joseph in for tea. Before taking a sip of the traditional drink, Joseph succumbs to sleep, and the two sisters do not disturb him until evening. Upon waking up, he apologizes, but the sisters had prepared a surprise dinner.

A week later, both sisters, Seo-Yeon and Mi-cha, departed together towards Seoul. Joseph accompanied them to the Honolulu airport, and they promised to stay in touch. Upon his return, he felt like he had closed a precious book. He should distance himself from those fond memories as he resumed his studies at the university, recalling the Japanese word "Giri," which represents the duty or pact of a scholarship recipient. Preoccupied with his work at Safeway, for Joseph, their faces gradually faded like a rainbow in Manoa Valley.

Chapter 15

Light in the basement

At the congratulatory reception organized by the Alliance Française of Hawaii for the recent graduates from the previous year, Joseph and Louise, having completed their stay in France, were invited to speak briefly to express their gratitude towards the organization and share their experiences in France. Joseph submitted his written report to the secretary, and Louise was expected to do the same in the coming days. During the event, Joseph had the opportunity to meet some French literature professors who were in attendance. At the end of the dinner, the professors approached him, inviting him to resume classes at the start of the new semester.

Ray, Michael's guitar teacher and close friend, had spent a few years as a student at the University of Hawaii. Before returning to Japan, he asked Michael and Joseph if they knew anyone looking for a small apartment. Thinking of his studies, Joseph volunteered to take his place before his departure. As the younger brother of Ray's best friend, Joseph met with the landlord, Mr. Suzuki, a Japanese-American man from Kaimuki. Joseph thus became the new tenant of a basement unit in a multi-story house. Though modest, this space was ideal for immersing himself for studying and reading his books. Wilhelmina Rise, the impressive straight road leading to the Kaimuki Ridge, was accessible by bike and cars through a few winding streets uphill. With his salary from Safeway supermarket, Joseph managed to afford the rent. He owned two bikes, one for daily commuting and the other for training with HBL members. Engrossed in the works of Céline,

Proust, Malraux, Gide, and Camus, Joseph became passionate about 20th-century literature. His basement, devoid of television and radio, was a true haven for reading his French books. At the age of 21, Joseph was now aiming to obtain his master's degree in French literature.

In front of the old white American house on stilts in Kaimuki, a brown cat slept in Hinata Bocco(basking in the sun) position, in the pleasant warmth, quite different from the rainy climate of their home deep in the Manoa Valley. A Jehovah's Witness representative came to talk to him in the garage as Joseph was dismounting his bicycle, back from the university. He was asked the name of the cat, and Joseph replied that his name was Marcel, as he was in the midst of reading "Swann's Way". With politeness, he declined the invitation to attend the Witness meeting, as he still had a stack of books to devour.

Chapter 16

Fishing

Joseph's father invited him on a fishing trip. After storing his bike in the laundry room, he helped load the equipment into the car. They stopped at the Diamond Head lookout where parking was available. Surfers with their boards could be seen descending the alley to the beach. Other surfers were in the ocean beyond the coral reef, waiting for the right wave, their silhouettes swaying up and down.

The fishing technique Joseph's father had mastered, called "dunking" in Hawaiian, involved baiting a hook with a piece of squid or octopus and casting it with the aid of a 2 or 3oz. weight. Once the fisherman felt the weight hit the bottom, he tightened the fishing line with the reel and placed his rod on the beach using a rod holder anchored in the sand. With four rods set up, they attached small bells to each rod to indicate which one had a bite. Joseph had to keep an eye on the rods while sharing drinks and the "bento" (picnic lunch) his mother had prepared.

While watching some surfers catching a wave, two of the rods they had set up bent, triggering the small bells. Joseph's father instructed him to take one, and they both managed to reel in 3 to 5-kilo bluefin trevally. They repeated the same actions about twenty minutes later, but Joseph's fish broke the bottom line on a rock in the depths and got away. With three fish in tow, the fishing trip came to an end, and they made their way back home carrying the rods, equipment, and cooler.

Joseph was beginning to enjoy fishing, but while he had managed to catch a fish, his brother Michael had already caught hundreds of different species. Just like in sports, he knew he could never reach the artistic fishing level of Michael or their father, both skilled anglers. They had ventured into fly fishing and found a prime spot with limited access for military personnel in Oahu's lagoon. They would leave home early in the morning and return before lunch, each having caught 4 or 5 exceptional-sized bonefish, while releasing each catch back into the lagoon. That was the art of fly fishing, with the philosophy of "catch and release".

During evenings with guests, Joseph's father would regale them with tales of his fishing exploits in Japan, particularly with the Nihon Masu (trout). He knew the rivers in the Kanto region well and would fly-fish for sizable trout. He recounted a story when his mother was in the hospital, and in between visits, to take his mind off things, he went fishing as she was due to give birth in a few days. He had spent the night in a ryokan (traditional Japanese inn), where the owner spoke of an enormous trout that no one had managed to catch because the fish was too clever, too capricious. While sipping green tea in the salon, his fingers touched the edges of a Zabuton, a cushion reinforced with golden silk threads at the corners. He took out his fishing knife and cut a few shiny filaments, attaching them to a fly. He cast this homemade fly onto the river's surface where he had seen the shadow of a fish, and suddenly, the massive trout struck, leaping out of the water. He said the moment he felt that fish, he knew he had a second son (Joseph), and when he brought his catch back to the ryokan, the owner couldn't believe his eyes. The monster was tamed and served on the evening's menu.

Chapter 17

Masi

During the holidays before the start of classes, Joseph made the most of his free time by cycling with his racing bike. He learned that the two-stage cycling race, the Haleiwa Sea Spree totaling 115 miles (185k) was being organized at the end of the month. Consequently, he rode more kilometers on each occasion, traveling from Kaimuki to Kailua. At the Bike Shop, he was advised to get a frame that fit him better because Joseph's "professional" bike seemed a bit too large. In ten days, a new racing bicycle from the Italian brand Masi arrived, prompting Joseph to sell the Raleigh Pro and acquire this new bike. This properly fitting racing bicycle inspired him once again to ride and explore new routes.

One day at the Bike Shop, he met a doctor who rode his bike every day from his home in Lanikai, passing through the intersection between Kaneohe and Kailua, riding up the Pali ascent and through the tunnel to get to work. Inspired by his story, Joseph set aside his fears to climb the hill and enter the tunnel despite the car horns, and descend Pali Highway at over 60 km/h. He was also inspired by a movie he had seen at the cinema, "Breaking Away," which depicted scenes of even more astonishing fast descents on the highways of California. Moreover, he had the same model of bicycle as in the film.

In 1972, the first edition of the race only had about forty riders, and Joseph participated in his first bike race. Two years later, nearly a hundred cyclists were registered, including a few women. Joseph's father provided transportation to Haleiwa, to the center of the village, and it was in front of Haleiwa Beach Park that the race began. The route circled part of Oahu, passing through the North Shore to the East Coast and following the long Kalanianaole Highway, finishing at Kapiolani Park, bordering the famous Waikiki Beach. The second stage would trace the route from Waikiki to Haleiwa, heading up Kunia Road. Joseph rode each stage at his own pace, trailing far behind the peloton of top cyclists, but he was happy to be able to participate once again in a major sporting event. A visiting foreigner won the race, a Dutchman, and Jim, the mechanic from the Bike Shop, came in second on the podium. As a memento of being a "finisher," Joseph received a cotton event logo patch, which he would have sewn onto his shorts.

Joseph's pride in his brother Michael was undeniable, even though he himself had never won trophies or stood on a podium. The memory of the Hawaii State High School Championships remained etched in his mind, where Michael, the sole representative of Roosevelt High School, qualified for the finals of the 180 yards low hurdles at the Punahou Track & Field stadium. Despite his small stature compared to the imposing competitor athletes from the other schools, Michael managed to secure the bronze medal, triggering tears of joy in Joseph looking on from the bleachers. This remarkable achievement not only strengthened the fraternal bond between the two brothers but also inspired Joseph to pursue a healthy and active life, continuing to maintain his fitness through his cycling outings. Michael's success remains a powerful reminder of what determination and hard work can accomplish, and Joseph carried this lesson with him in his own adventures.

Chapter 18

Acoustic

The school year began slowly for Joseph, with the constant thought of the Korean sisters on his mind. He imagined that they missed the daily gestures and the island lifestyle, and for him, they were missed every day. The image of Seo Yeon returned: tapping the pavement with her cane and expressing herself through her violin, mastering musical scores. At Records Hawaii, he searched for some Mozart, Mendelssohn, Vivaldi, and Beethoven LPs, and he listened to them during his breaks from reading on his Hi-Fi. Before meeting Seo Yeon, he only listened to the English group, The Beatles, Rock and Roll, and a few Blues records that his brother had in his collection at home. Mi-cha's letters, written in fine handwriting and received once or twice a month, informed him about their mother's health in their old house in Seoul. Seo Yeon was practicing diligently hoping to join the university orchestra, and Mi-cha was waiting for news about a position in a downtown law firm. Their father hired a maid to take care of their mother during their absences.

Ray, the former tenant, had entrusted his record collection and stereo system to Michael. Upon visiting the room Ray had left behind for Joseph, Michael, surprised by the tight space and piles of books, gifted him the records he already owned along with the stereo system and a pair of headphones. With the headphones, Joseph could listen to music without disturbing anyone nearby, respecting both the neighbors and the landlord. Taking a break from reading the French books, Joseph would doze off with his headphones on, listening to piano and violin sonatas, thinking of Seo-Yeon.

Ike, Joseph's Japanese friend from Safeway, had returned to Japan a few months before Joseph's return from France. Joseph missed him, but it was also an opportunity for him to focus on his studies. While his "sempai" (mentor) was friendly, he was also a heavy drinker, often taking Joseph to various bars and restaurants in Honolulu and returning around 1 a.m. If Joseph had a few glasses of wine or a gin and tonic, Ike could continue sipping Jack Daniels all night long. Fortunately, Joseph's other mentor, Greg the surfer, was in the same philosophy class, and as they studied existentialism, they shared interests in reading Beckett, Sartre, and Camus. They often found themselves on the bench during their breaks at Safeway, engaging in philosophical discussions. One day, Greg expressed a desire to learn to play the guitar. Joseph offered to teach him a few chords and invited him to bring his guitar to his place in Kaimuki.

As Greg progressed on the guitar, Joseph suggested they learn a few songs together with their two acoustic guitars. They delved into the musical world of Neil Young and Bob Dylan, with Greg taking on the vocals. Respecting their neighbors, Joseph remembered the soundproof rehearsal rooms at the university that he had discovered with Seo-Yeon. The Orvis rooms were also available in the evenings, and they found that most of them were free in the evenings. Rehearsing the same songs several times a week, Greg dared to ask the owner of Mama Mia's Pizza if the duo could perform for their audience soon. The cozy Italian bistro was located in Puck's Alley, a popular spot among students, offering shops, organic products in the Health Food Store, and a few restaurants with reasonable prices, situated at the intersection of University Avenue and South King Street.

Michael continued to progress in music by acquiring a new electric guitar, the Gibson Les Paul. He formed a Rock 'n Roll band called Frosted Glass, which became one of the most sought-after groups in

Oahu, whether for private parties or outdoor concerts at Sandy Beach. It was the post-Woodstock era, and outdoor concerts in the vast space of Diamond Head crater became popular.

Over time, the duo Joseph and Greg performed at Mama Mia's one Friday night with a repertoire of a dozen songs. Despite Joseph's mixed feelings, sensing it was a failure, the audience offered some applause. Seeing his singing friend with a smile, Joseph silently supported him, enjoying the dinner and drinks provided by the owner.

Following their unsuccessful performance, the two friends found themselves several times a month attending concerts by visiting artists in Hawaii, such as Jethro Tull, Grateful Dead and Jefferson Starship. Greg was a big fan of Ian Anderson and furthered his musical prowess by acquiring a flute, much like the Jethro Tull frontman. While Ike was an alcoholic, Greg preferred beer and marijuana. Joseph had already experimented with weed in high school, but he didn't partake regularly, limiting those moments to occasions with friends. He wondered if this could be the reason their musical venture wasn't progressing, or if they simply lacked the innate creativity of true musicians.

His thoughts turned to Seo-Yeon and her remarkable ability to memorize musical scores using Braille, which she expressed through the violin. When she played, it seemed as though her emotions soared, through the music of ancient composers from a distant era. Joseph realized that in music, he was like a poverty stricken child, unable to read or write, simply listening to the world around him. Despite his secret desire to board a plane to South Korea and confront his own limits, he kept this dream within himself, continuing to learn new songs with Greg.

Before the end of the semester, Greg reveals to Joseph his imminent surprise: his departure for South Korea. Tempted to swap roles to fulfill his own dream, Joseph learns that his friend has enlisted in the US Army, becoming an American soldier for several years. His goal was to benefit from the GI Bill, which offers tuition-free education at the end of his military contract. As a non-native of Hawaii, Greg's tuition fees were prohibitive, and he found this solution. His first assignment would place him in the Demilitarized Zone between South Korea and North Korea. Recently married to Sharie, Greg had chosen Joseph as his best man at their wedding. The newlyweds agreed on post-military arrangements that would facilitate their life together in the years to come. Greg's departure leaves Joseph with a sense of solitude, prompting him to focus even more on his studies.

Chapter 19

Music and memories

Comforted by the classical music he listened to with his headphones, Joseph sometimes reminisced about his childhood. During the summer, they would take the insect nets out of the garage closet to chase and catch cicadas, dragonflies and butterflies. The parents provided shadow boxes and preservation kits for both Michael and Joseph. The older brother, always more agile, would fill his box with singing cicadas, emitting a soft "min min min" like a melody. These creatures emerged from the ground after seventeen years to offer a second refrain on another octave. Their wings were transparent and delicate, resembling those of dragonflies, and were featured in Michael's box.

Joseph's box contained brown cicadas producing a strange buzzing noise. The brown cicadas were easier to catch as they were found on poles or walls. However, the other cicadas would perch on tree branches, too high for Joseph. Michael, the agile athlete, could easily climb trees. Another cicada, as small as a cricket, sang a kind of serenade "Oh...shiiii tsuku tsuku tsuku tsuku tsuku" for several minutes, ending with a pleading cry "O shiii o shiiii, o shiii o shiii!" The butterflies, more delicate to catch, had fragile wings that broke easily, eliciting Joseph's compassion for these frail creatures.

Inspired by the year he spent in France, Joseph immersed himself in reading, dedicating hours between classes at the university library. He obtained his Bachelor of Arts degree in 1975, then continued his studies in French literature. The reading, sometimes challenging as in

Proust's "In Search of Lost Time," was supported by the devoted passion of his literature professors. After the new year holidays, Joseph declined the job offer at the supermarket to focus on the challenging exams. He successfully passed the final exam with honors, earning his Master's degree in French literature.

Joseph's horizon expanded when he was invited to attend a presentation by a hotel manager and his colleagues from Tahiti. Captivated by the exceptional Polynesian landscapes showcased in a slideshow, Joseph volunteered for an interview with the hotel manager. Among his peers, he was selected to work in Tahiti, thus opening a new chapter in his journey.

Chapter 20

Iaorana

His arrival at Faa'a Airport, aboard the Pan Am flight from Honolulu to Papeete, marks the beginning of his job as reception manager at the Hotel Tahara'a in Tahiti in the summer of 1976. From his hotel room window, Joseph gazes out at the view of Matavai Bay. The azure sky is dotted with a few cumulus clouds, and the vastness of the Pacific Ocean stretches as far as the eye can see. In the distance, he sees small waves breaking over the fringing reef of the Taaone lagoon. The Tahara'a signifies One Tree Hill, the historical site where 18th-century explorers came to Tahiti to observe the passage of the planet Venus. Feeling a sense of déjà vu, he senses a similarity with the islands of Hawaii. Was this the Hawaii that Joseph's father had known in his youth?

Most of the employees are Tahitians, and they call him "Tinito"(Chinese) due to his origin. His mission is to replace the Japanese receptionist Takashi, whose contract was up at the end of the year. A weekly direct flight from Air France between Tokyo and Papeete ensures the regular arrival of Japanese tourists. The Assistant manager, Lionel, accompanies him to show him his room, and he notices a fishing rod in one corner. Lionel asks if he enjoys fishing, and although he doesn't, Joseph tells him it's to please his father, who is passionate about fishing in Hawaii. Unpacking his belongings, he takes the bicycle frame out of the box and assembles the wheels. He takes the elevator to the 1st floor, towards the reception. As the hotel is built on a cliff, the floors are reversed, and Joseph rolls his bicycle on the green carpet, eliciting astonished looks from the Polynesian employees. At the porte cochère, an immense carved wooden tiki surveys all. He takes his first ride towards the east coast of Tahiti. His Campagnolo equipment, tubular tires, 52-42 chainrings, and 5-speed cassette remind him of his bike races in Hawaii. He passes through the municipalities of Mahina and Papenoo, noticing a Chinese supermarket with the name Jissang, reminiscent of "ji-san," meaning "old man" in Japanese, evoking his childhood in Japan.

Joseph's grandfather, nicknamed Jissan by adults and oji-chan familiarly by children, remained a mysterious figure. A former carpenter, he used his skills to create useful objects for the vast house in the heart of Tokyo, in Akasaka. One of his creations was a small pond in the garden, housing freshwater fish such as goldfish, as well as 'koi' or carp measuring up to 30 centimeters. Joseph harbored a certain apprehension towards his grandfather, as he was rather silent.

During "Omatsuri"(festival) in summer, "Oba-chan"(Grandmother) would accompany the children to the Shinto shrine Nogi Jinja, where they would participate in traditional games and admire the fireworks. Michael, Joseph and Susanne would dress up in "yukata" (lightweight kimono) and walk with getas(wooden sandals) click clacking on the pavement. One of their favorite games was fishing for small goldfish with paper-mâché scoops. Joseph would content himself with catching the smallest fish, the "medaka"(oryzias), as his scoop would easily tear upon contact with the fish tank water. Michael on the other hand would always be able to catch a few nice goldfish. At the end of the evening, everyone would leave with a plastic bag filled with water, tied with a ribbon, containing the caught fish, ready to find their place in the pond. Grandmother never forgot to procure amulets from the temple each offering safety, good health, or fortune. Before returning home, the children were treated to pink cotton candy, a delicious, sweet touch to these festive moments.

During his days off at the Tahara'a Hotel, Joseph savored his moments of freedom by exploring various places on the island by bike. His journey led him to complete the Island Tour, an adventure that occupied most of his day. During his stops at small pandanus shelters, he indulged in watermelons, mangoes, bananas, and papayas, tropical fruits that cost only a few hundred French Polynesian francs. The Polynesian vendors, often mothers with their babies, expressed their gratitude, creating warm encounters with Tahitian families with dark brown complexions.

Feeling fit, Joseph continued his journey on his 10-speed Masi bicycle. Equipped with a velvet bag under the saddle, given as a gift with the purchase of a Crown Royal whisky, covering the spare tire in case of a puncture, he was ready for adventure. Unfortunately, in Papara, misfortune struck with a flat tire, but he managed to change the tubular tire with the equipment at his disposal. However, between Pirae and Arue, the front wheel suffered another puncture. With no spare left, Joseph contemplated walking with his bike when fate smiled upon him. A generous driver of a "Deux Chevaux"(2 Horsepower) car stopped, offering to drive him by dismantling the bike to load it. Thus, he was brought back to the Tahara'a, marking the end of an unforgettable day of adventure.

During his bike rides, Joseph encountered imposing cyclists proudly displaying Polynesian tattoos on their legs and arms. Invited to join the Orohena club, a local cycling association, he participated in some training sessions with club members and engaged in road bike races. The differences from his cycling experiences in Hawaii were quickly apparent. Races in Tahiti were more aggressive, and despite his efforts to stay in the peloton, Joseph often found himself lagging behind after about twenty kilometers, especially in races of sixty kilometers or more.

At lunch with the staff at the Hotel Tahara'a, the accountant, nicknamed "Gazzo," noticed Joseph whilst reading La Dépêche de

Tahiti newspaper, open on his broad chest. Gazzo teasingly remarked to Joseph about his ninth place in the race. Joseph, a mixture of embarrassment and pride, offered a smile without offering any explanations, grateful for having taken part in these local competitions.

Chapter 21

Fronto Pronto

Joseph established himself as the Rooms Division Manager, acting as the Front Office Manager after a few months since his arrival. Under the guidance of Lionel, a former Australian professional musician who had found his calling in hotel management at the Hotel Tahara'a, Joseph learned the ins and outs of the industry. Takashi, ensuring that his replacement did not make similar mistakes to his own, also provided guidance. The environment was pleasant, surrounded by charming Polynesian women, as Antoinette, in charge of the reservations desk with Somsri from Thailand, Verna and Christine Tahitian-Chinese ladies in the accounting office, and receptionists like Ruth from New Zealand and cashier Tapita from Rarotonga. Joseph particularly appreciated that everyone spoke French as well as English, offering a different atmosphere from Hawaii where English predominated.

Takashi, in Japan had expressed his desire to work in Tahiti through numerous letters before getting hired to work at the Tahara'a. Three years older than Joseph, Takashi was a dedicated athlete, known for his good grasp of English. Often seen with a paperback book in English, he added an international touch to the hotel environment. Passionate about surfing, he would load his board into his box like Fiat car and regularly head to Papenoo, a surfer's haven where wave enthusiasts awaited the perfect swell. Takashi, also a tennis enthusiast, engaged in matches on the court next to the hotel's large parking lot. His athletic commitment even extended to jogging, descending the

Tahara'a hill to Taone and returning halfway up while running. In addition to all this, Takashi was a charmer, sharing his experiences with Joseph, the innocent one, and suggesting he do the same.

Joseph also found pleasure in conversing in Japanese with the hotel guests. He befriended the guides of Japanese groups, often composed of ten couples or more. An intriguing situation arose when Takashi, before the arrival of a group, approached him, having carefully studied the list of names in the reservation file. He asked Joseph to assign a room with an exceptional view to two women mentioned, referring to them as "O.L." or Office Ladies. Listening to Takashi's speech, Joseph discovered that they were young single women, colleagues in the same company, going on vacation together, taking advantage of the enticing group fare. During their stay, Joseph observed Takashi walking towards the lobby talking to one of the women, with a big smile. Incredulous, Joseph preferred to immerse himself in his romantic memories on Oahu.

With his earnings from work, Joseph had acquired an old used car, a convertible Karmann Ghia. Inviting Takashi for a tour around the island, they stopped at a red light in Taone, a few kilometers from downtown Papeete. It was Takashi who first noticed smoke coming from the hood, and the car stopped moving. Putting the car in neutral, they pushed it to the amusement of other drivers, off the main road. Takashi knew a mechanic, a certain Fred of New Zealand origin, whom he had already taken his Fiat to. Luckily, the garage was 500 meters from where they were, and they began pushing the car again.

Takashi had accrued his annual leave days before Joseph's arrival, and he decided to take a trip to South America. Joseph's car was running again, and he dropped him off at Faa'a Airport while noting the return flight on Lan Chile. Four weeks later, Joseph picked him up at the airport. As Takashi got into the car, he was in a joyous mood, announcing that he was getting married. At first, Joseph thought it was a joke. Two weeks later, Takashi introduced his future wife, a lovely young Argentine named Anna, and they planned to marry at the town hall in Arue. Joseph then understood that in addition to English, Takashi was also was quite fluent in the Spanish language.

Chapter 22

Staying in Contact

Two years had passed, and Joseph continued to receive letters from Mi-Cha, written on behalf of Seo-Yeon. The correspondence had become less frequent, with a letter every two or three months. The shared news was filled with congratulations for Joseph's work in Tahiti. The sisters' mother was doing better, more rooted in her heritage, although her memory showed signs of decline. A maid was present full-time to ensure their well-being. Mi-Cha had found a position in a law firm focused on international clientele, working as a full-time secretary-interpreter. As for Seo-Yeon, she had been recognized by a pianist from the orchestra, Hana, a former classmate, and the two had become very close friends. Hana, learning that Mi-Cha was often busy with work, had arranged things with the family to become Seo-Yeon's primary caregiver, and together they practiced their instruments in the university rehearsal room.

In his reply letter, Joseph includes a few postcards, notably one featuring an aerial view of the Tahara'a Hotel perched on a cliff. He indicates the location of his room with an arrow-shaped sticker. He summarizes some anecdotes from his arrival, shares the warm welcome from the Polynesians, and discusses his work. Joseph describes the similarity of the landscapes to those of Oahu. After posting his letter at the Post and Telecommunications Office in Papeete, he retrieves his bike secured to a pole. Joseph reflects on the constant darkness that Seo-Yeon must face daily. He feels some tears of guilt, realizing he had taken for granted the gift of sight.

JOSEPH IS SURPRISED by the next letter, as the handwriting was different. It was Hana, the friend and caregiver who would now write on behalf of Seo-Yeon. Mi-cha had met an American on a business trip to Seoul, representing a telecommunications company. After several dates, they had become inseparable. Their marriage was arranged for next month. Hana remembered the sisters from school, in physical education and music classes. During a school competition, they all stood on the podium for swimming in the 50m freestyle event. Six months later, in winter, Hana had heard about the skiing accident at school. She hadn't seen Seo-Yeon in a long time, as Hana and her family had moved to Busan. Reconnecting with Seo-Yeon in the same orchestra, they renewed their friendship, and Hana felt it was her duty to help her friend. Joseph was also impressed by the way Hana wrote, addressing him with gratitude, using honorific terms, a form of Asian politeness he had forgotten. In Tahiti, on the other hand, everyone addressed each other casually.

Joseph arranged for a bouquet of flowers to be sent for Mi-Cha's wedding through FTD at a florist in Papeete. Although he was invited to the wedding in Seoul, work obligations prevented him from leaving his post. He received the letter with some photos of the wedding two weeks later. Mi-Cha and Steven warmly thanked Joseph for the flowers from Tahiti. Steven, originally from San Francisco, worked in New York. The wedding ceremony took place at Myeongdong Cathedral in Seoul. At the reception, in one of the banquet rooms of the Grand Hyatt, guests enjoyed a gourmet dinner. Seo-Yeon and Hana surprised everyone by performing a sonata for violin and piano by Mozart, dedicated to the newlyweds.

Chapter 23

Taponé be careful

John, a surfer from Hawaii, joined the reception team at Tahara'a. This Japanese-American stood at 1.8 meters tall with chestnut hair. During staff meetings led by Joseph, discussing the day's arrivals and departures or the week's forecasts, his eyes often turned to the waves of Matavai Bay, always seeking the perfect wave to surf. Knowing that Joseph also had Japanese roots, John proposed a fishing trip with Hawaiian spears at the base of the Tahara'a cliff. The idea was to search for fish or octopus in the fringing reef, usually found in coral crevices.

It was nearing the end of the year and Japanese tradition also common in Hawaii, involves feasting on seafood during the holidays. Walking with rubber sandals, with their fins, mask and snorkel in a pandanus basket, they advanced along the narrow trail at the edge of the cliff. Holding their Hawaiian sling spears, they waded through the clear lagoon for nearly ten minutes, between the rocks in front of the reef, in water waist deep. Suddenly, John exclaimed, "Look at that set", and Joseph, not understanding surfer jargon, was confused. "Set" refers to the rise of waves that brings a series of seven waves, and John shouted for him to quickly climb the cliff. Running, they reached the cliff and began to climb. However, the sound of the first huge wave crashing on the reef frightened him, and suddenly, white foam enveloped them. Joseph was torn from the cliff, finding himself in the middle of the small lagoon between the rocks. Fortunately, he was able to stabilize himself, his spear anchored between the rocks providing him balance. Not seeing his friend and facing a strong current, he felt a white terror shaking him from side to side. After a long minute, he spotted John who shouted, "Run," and they dashed along the narrow path below the cliff, running to the beach.

A week later, they rode Joseph's Yamaha 175cc, with their fishing gear strapped to their shoulders in the pandanus basket and the two Hawaiian spears balanced on the motorcycle's handlebars. Opting for the west coast, they stumbled upon the old Tahiti Village in the commune of Punaauia, with a few bungalows lining a beautiful beach. After parking the motorcycle in a lot, they took an adjacent trail. Their goal, the same as before, was to catch some fish and octopus to celebrate the new year. Equipped with masks, snorkels and fins, within fifteen minutes they could reach a coral formation, about a hundred meters within the barrier reef.

Joseph observed groups of red and yellow striped snappers, soldierfish, as well as other colorful and shimmering species. John, particularly skilled with the Hawaiian sling spear, began to catch a few fish. However, Joseph could not hold his breath long enough to stay among the rocks where the fish sought refuge. John indicated he would continue toward the reef and return later. Feeling demotivated and without any fish, Joseph decided to head back. Midway, he discovered a rock with an octopus near its hole, which he managed to catch with his spear. It was a real challenge to put the octopus in his mesh diving bag while swimming simultaneously. On his way back, he spotted another octopus and captured it with more difficulty, as it had retreated deep into its hole. After several dives to catch his breath, he managed the situation with the spear and succeeded in placing the prey in his bag. Satisfied not to return empty-handed, he began swimming back to the beach.

However, after a few minutes, Joseph realized he wasn't making any progress. He was going around in circles, caught in a cross-current. Not being a strong swimmer, panic set in. Scanning the beach, he spotted John, already back, signaling for him to swim in a direction he indicated with his hands, understanding his difficulty. Following the surfer's instructions, he once again escaped drowning. With the octopus and John's selection of fish, they were ready to celebrate the New Year for a festive weekend.

Chapter 24

Komapsumnida

Joseph was slightly taken aback by the contents of the letter from Hana, written before Easter. While still maintaining a respectful tone, Hana shared some personal details this time. In Busan, she had worked for a travel agency as a marketing agent for destinations. She was responsible for drafting brochures and met the editor of the press house. Following a few friendly outings, they got married, with a honeymoon in Hawaii. Initially, it was paradise, but a few months later, she discovered her husband's gambling addiction in various casinos, often returning after 2:00 a.m., disheveled. In addition to this, she endured her husband's violent side, leaving bruises on her body. Hana later filed for divorce, and the judge granted the legal separation, allowing her to leave Busan and return to Seoul. After her ordeal with the terrible man, she resigned herself to a solitary life. She found an apartment and was looking for work when she saw a job listing at the university for a piano teacher position. The faculty later invited her to join the orchestra, and it was during their first gathering of musicians that she recognized Seo-Yeon. Hana promised to always be by Seo-Yeon's side from now on and not to worry. She confessed that their constant closeness had awakened feelings she had not yet experienced towards a woman. In closing, she politely apologized to Joseph, assuring him that he would always be in Seo-Yeon's heart.

Joseph, happy and sad, responded by expressing his compassion and support. He is proud to know these two courageous women, wishing them happiness and peace. He imagines their sonata infused with deep emotions, promising to listen to classical music while thinking of them. Sharing an anecdote about his outing with Rita and the discovery of her relationship with her cousin Laura, Joseph mentions the coincidence of seeing Laura as a Pan Am flight stewardess during a transit stay at the Hotel Tahara'a. The hotel administration had a contract with Pan Am as well as Lan Chile for their crew layovers. Joseph invited his friend from Safeway, for a day of exploring the island of Moorea. He recalls the shared happiness felt while understanding Laura's preferences. Joseph closes by thanking Hana for taking good care of his first love. As he listens to a Mozart sonata for violin and piano, he thinks of Seo-Yeon and Hana, hoping for their well-being together.

Memories bring him back to his days working at Safeway supermarket in Manoa, where a friendly atmosphere prevailed among the staff. Rita, Laura, Beverly, Patricia, Carl, Keith, and others formed a small family, working in various departments of the store. The warm interaction with customers created pleasant moments of conversation, marked by mutual smiles. Joseph admired how Rita and Laura knew the customers by their names.

For the staff party carefully organized by Rita, Joseph decided to cycle there. He was accompanied by Carl, the dairy products manager, on a 30-kilometer journey to Kailua. Despite several stops to allow Carl to keep up, they successfully arrived at the park. However, Carl, exhausted, humorously declared that Joseph was "crazy." The day included games and a barbecue lunch, with prizes adding to the general joy. Management expressed satisfaction, thanking all employees for their teamwork and the success of the day. It was in this supermarket that Joseph acquired various aspects of hospitality, an experience he would carry with him in his work in Tahiti.

Chapter 25

Sempai

Over time, Joseph forged friendly bonds with the staff at Hotel Tahara'a, turning this team into his small family abroad. Lionel, the assistant manager from Australia, became his guide in the art of fishing. With ten years senior to Joseph, Lionel was his "sempai" (mentor), and Joseph, his "kohai" (pupil). Before work, at dawn, Joseph would seek out Lionel on his Yamaha motorcycle, and together, they would head to Mahina Beach, opposite Motu Martin, for a morning fishing session. They walked on the black sand in silence, carrying their rods, noticing the current flowing in the channel between the beach and the motu (islet).

Lionel taught Joseph the delicate art of lure casting with a fishing rod, handling the reel and the monofilament line. On the beach, they observed a Tahitian fisherman, nicknamed Pete the Purist. The Tahitian man fished without a rod or reel, simply using a nylon line and baited hook, swirling his bait around his head and casting it about twenty meters from the shore.

One day, as Lionel wrestled with an impressive catch, Joseph, respectful, quickly reeled in his lure and line to give him more space. It was a 12-kilo bluefin trevally, which Lionel proudly displayed upon their return on the motorcycle, eliciting surprise from an early morning pedestrian who was seeking fresh baguettes at the Venus Star store.

At the workplace, meetings in Lionel's office often extended beyond professional matters, delving into subjects like music. Lionel, who had started in Tahiti as a professional musician with a jazz band, had played in renowned clubs such as Poro Plage, Hotel Tahiti, and Lafayette before taking on the role of Assistant Manager. Their discussions covered a wide range, from Rock & Roll to the Beatles, and Joseph expanded his knowledge on jazz artists less familiar to him.

Joseph noticed a chessboard on Lionel's desk, and upon discovering that Lionel was a former regional chess champion at during his school years, he was intrigued. He learned that Lionel regularly played with an American journalist, Al, the editor of Tahiti Sun Press. They would phone each other every day before noon to make a move. Lionel, with a smile, confessed that most of the time, he emerged victorious. He explained that he visualized the chessboard in his mind, enabling him to play even as the pieces were often in disarray on his desk, his office cleaned daily by Housekeeping, without ever disrupting the flow of the mental game.

The bond between Joseph and his sempai Lionel extended beyond work-related topics, as in a shared passion for reading. Lionel, an avid book enthusiast, often lent books to Joseph covering a wide range of subjects, from history to chess strategy, contemporary bestsellers to music and cinema. Their preferred space for discussing these topics was the management dining room, where they regularly shared the same table during breakfast and lunch.

Takashi, joining them around 12:30 after working the night shift, placed his order, and Lionel, with a touch of humor, would ask him if he was really hungry having seen him earlier for breakfast. Takashi, in a blend of sincerity and humor, would invariably reply that he wasn't really hungry but didn't want to miss a meal. A light and pleasant dynamic animated their shared moments at the hotel.

Chapter 26

Romantica

Daily encounters with locals, whether Tahitian or Japanese, was expected at the reception. These individuals welcomed guests at Faa'a International Airport and escorted them to the hotel, presenting their vouchers or excursion packages. Joseph, an admirer of one of the Japanese guides named Yukie, boldly invited her to dinner in Papeete. The rendezvous at La Petite Auberge restaurant began with Joseph patiently waiting, enjoying an aperitif before the agreed-upon time. Yukie, an independent and charming woman with her hair tied in a bun, arrived ten minutes late, apologizing politely. Their dinner in this small French restaurant proved delightful, accompanied by a shared bottle of Chardonnay. After desserts and coffee, they rose to leave, pleased with their encounter, setting a date for their next dinner.

L'Api'zeria, located across from the waterfront of Papeete, offered an Italian menu in a rustic atmosphere adorned with a panoramic fresco like painting depicting an Italian village. Yukie arrived a few minutes late, but Joseph was delighted to see her smiling. The delicious meal was accompanied by a bottle of Saint-Émilion. Yukie confided in Joseph that during her two years in Papeete, she had some relationships with French men, but it was the first time she felt comfortable speaking Japanese. On his part, Joseph mentioned his hesitations regarding Japanese women, fearing they wouldn't understand him. After the meal, Yukie suggested that Joseph follow her car on his motorcycle. In the dimly lit atmosphere of her apartment, illuminated by a lamp adorned with butterflies, time seemed suspended during their first kiss. Yukie untied her bun, letting her silky black hair fall to her shoulders.

Yukie was also active with her friends, and one weekend, she picked up Joseph by car to spend time at her friend Karine's place, a French woman from Nice who practiced pottery in Punaauia. Upon arrival at Karine's, she was preparing the equipment for water skiing. Her boat was moored at the pontoon at their neighbor's property on the waterfront. Joseph admitted he had never tried this sport before, but with Yukie's impromptu lessons and Karine's guidance driving the boat, he managed to stand up and follow the boat. Witnessing Karine and Yukie's acrobatic movements in turn, Joseph was amazed by their talent. Upon return, after storing the equipment, Karine started the barbecue while Joseph and Yukie showered. Discovering the steaks that Karine had seasoned, Joseph forgot to inform Yukie that he was vegetarian. Seeing his concern and guilty look, Yukie assured him not to worry, as Karine had a piece of Mahi Mahi that she brought out for the feast, and she had also prepared a delicious Niçoise salad. It was a day rich in new experiences and camaraderie.

Chapter 27

Déjà vu

During the school holidays, Joseph hired a Frenchman, Damien, to work as a receptionist. His English was proficient, as he was a teacher at Mahina Elementary School. His goal was to improve his English by working full-time for a few months. Damien was curious about the Japanese-American who spoke Japanese, English, and French. He frequently invited Joseph to lunch or dinner with him and his friends at gourmet restaurants in Papeete.

Damien was well-dressed, wearing tinted glasses, and showed generosity by covering all the expenses for meals and drinks. His car was a Mercedes, but he appeared modest. Pierre, who worked at the cash register, also knew Damien, as they had taken the same mathematics courses in high school. Upon learning that Pierre had obtained his pilot's license, Damien came up with the idea of organizing a getaway, with a maiden flight for Joseph. On board the small Piper aircraft, Joseph sat next to Pierre while Damien sat in the back. Joseph was fascinated by all the instruments, including the altimeter, and the various panels that Pierre mastered. The takeoff from Faaa Airport in the small plane was impressive as it gained altitude, and Joseph looked out at the landscape of Tahiti, with buildings and houses becoming tiny specks below.

Pierre had booked a night in Rangiroa at a 'pension' or guest house, knowing that the plane would not be needed until the following afternoon with the Aero Club de Tahiti. The trio, carrying just a small bag with a few spare clothes, found shelter in the modest, but large family house.

Due to his regular visits, Pierre was considered like a member of this welcoming Tahitian family. Lunch was an exquisite culinary experience, featuring the 'poisson cru' (raw fish) a Polynesian ceviche like specialty, various grilled fish, and the delicious "pahua" (clams) served in a curry sauce.

Having brought his fishing rod, Joseph intended to try catching some fish during their exploration of the vast lagoon. They waded in the crystalline lagoon among the rocks and corals. Upon reaching the edge of the reef, about twenty meters from the lagoon Joseph stood on a large rock between the lagoon and the sea, casting his lure while his friends snorkeled. Three fish followed the lure, and he managed to catch one. It was an incredible experience to see so many reef fish in transparent water under the vast blue sky with a few clouds on the horizon.

Joseph found himself in an unexpected situation at work one day when Christine from accounting wanted to share something interesting with him. She took him aside to a quiet corner and advised him to be cautious of Damien. When he asked her why, she confided in him that she suspected Damien sometimes wore a wig. Although Joseph initially laughed it off, he began to notice Damien's gaze often drifting towards Pierre's face. However, Pierre was already in a relationship with one of the lovely receptionists, Stella. Confused and surprised by Christine's revelation, Joseph thanked her and the next day, he indeed noticed that Damien's hairstyle seemed a bit odd.

It had been a while since Joseph had seen Yukie, and she seemed constantly busy with her work at the agency. Nearly two months had passed since their last dinner together at the Auberge du Pacifique in Punaauia. She took Joseph by surprise by announcing her imminent departure. Yukie had rekindled a past relationship, and she had been invited to accompany her partner to France. With a mix of emotions, she proudly showed off her brand new engagement ring. Though Joseph felt sadness, he offered Yukie his support and compassion as she embarked on this new chapter of her life.

Chapter 28

Bora Bora

Arriving on the enchanting island of Bora Bora for his annual leave, Joseph was greeted by a breathtaking landscape. The Hotel Bora Bora, established in 1961, stood as a symbol of luxury offering the first overwater bungalows on the island, that became iconic to the destination. Nestled between two stretches of white sand, separated by Point Raititi, the hotel provided an idyllic setting.

Joseph, mesmerized by the natural beauty surrounding him, marveled at the majestic Mount Otemanu and the crystal-clear lagoon that defied any description as his Air Polynésie plane descended. The magic of Bora Bora continued during the one hour journey to the main island, aboard the picturesque shuttle providing breathtaking views. Welcomed by the warm smile of Fredo, a local Tahitian, Joseph settled into the bumpy « le truck » ride that took him along the dirt road. He admired the coconut trees lining the route, the lagoon with its infinite shades of blue, and the vast, unyielding sky, offering a unique experience in the beauty of French Polynesia.

His reception at the hotel, was a warm welcome by the management, a group of American expatriates, and a few Tahitian receptionists. As he sipped on a refreshing coconut water, he was informed that the hotel was fully booked, but he would be accommodated in Samantha's residence, a Japanese-American from Hawaii who had been working in the office for six months. The encounter with Samantha was memorable, with her long black hair that reached her waist.

After a casual lunch, Joseph expressed his desire to rent one of the available bikes, but the receptionist informed him that they were all already reserved by guests. It was then that Samantha, upon learning that Joseph was an avid cyclist in Tahiti, generously offered him the use of her own personal bike during his stay. Without hesitation, Joseph accepted the offer and mounted the "lady's" bike to explore the island's roads, discovering breathtaking landscapes along the unpaved coastal route. It was an adventure that promised unforgettable discoveries at every turn.

Equipped with a set of mask, snorkel and fins, Joseph plunged into the lagoon in front of the bungalows, discovering an underwater ecosystem rich in marine life and bursts of color. Schools of shimmering tropical fish, blue jacks, rays, and even a turtle gracefully navigated just a few meters from the shore. The underwater scene unfolded with a natural magic that reminded Joseph of his first snorkeling experience at Hanauma Bay on Oahu.

He also noticed that the Polynesians working at the reception, restaurant, and beach bar were notably more laid-back than their counterparts in Tahiti. Joseph appreciated their kindness and smiles, adding a touch of friendliness to his already enchanting stay.

During his second exploration of the island, Joseph made a stop at the small gas station in front of the Chin Lee grocery store, established in 1934 by a Chinese couple. Wanting to inflate his tires to avoid a flat, the Chinese man generously offered the use of the air compressor. Joseph noticed the limited number of cars on the island, learning that there were only about a dozen, but that motorized two-wheelers, especially Piaggio Vespa scooters, were popular. As he rode away on his bike, Joseph inwardly promised to return soon to this magical island that had captivated his heart.

The vacation week came to an end, and Joseph expressed his deep gratitude to the management, staff, and especially to Samantha for lending him her bike. Craig, the purchasing manager, teased Joseph, asking if he had found happiness in the company of "Sam," but Joseph assured him that their relationship was simply friendly and platonic. Upon returning to Tahiti, an important decision had matured within him: to request an immediate transfer to work in Bora Bora.

Chapter 29

Tiarei

With his bike, Joseph rediscovers the landscapes of the East Coast of Tahiti. A small climb called Nivée offers a rapid descent towards the commune of Tiarei, and he discovers a long rocky shoreline where the ocean waves crash against the fissures of the ancient volcanic coast. Joseph contemplates these fissures and observes how the current forces the water onto the rocks, hiding them from view and then exposing them again as it recedes. The blowhole is at the end of this long straight line, spitting out white foam, sometimes reaching the road. He recalls the south eastern coast of Oahu, where similar rock formations exist, between Hanauama Bay and Sandy Beach, where he had raced down the descent on his bicycle at high speed. In the distance, he would notice a few Hawaiian fishermen, their rods anchored in holes with their rod holders.

At the Hotel Tahara'a, Joseph suggests to his sempai Lionel to go fishing in Tiare. Remembering how his father used to prepare his hooks, leaders, and weights to effectively fish among the rocks and coral reef off Diamond Head, Joseph explains to Lionel this fishing technique called "dunking." Since Lionel is not familiar with this style of fishing, Joseph decides to go on his bicycle to the Nauti-Sport store at Fare Ute to find the curved hooks called "Tankichi," the leaders, and the necessary weights. With his material in his backpack, he climbs up the hill of Tahara'a with a lightness in his legs, eager to share this fishing experience with Lionel.

A crucial detail was missing for this fishing trip: the bait. After searching in several stores, Joseph finally finds some frozen raw squid at the supermarket in Arue. He then heads to Lionel's place in Mahina, and together, riding on his Yamaha motorcycle, they make their way to their new adventure. Arriving at an ideal spot in Tiare, they begin to prepare their gear on the roadside. They also brought along some beers and found a packet of joints left behind by guests in one of the rooms. As the day is just beginning and the sky is clearing, heralding a beautiful sunny day, Lionel, not having brought a cooler, expresses his displeasure at the thought of drinking warm beer. So, he cracks open his can, and Joseph follows suit. Upon discovering the "gift" left by the guests, Lionel lights up a joint, which he shares with his kohai. Under the influence of alcohol and weed, the two fishermen realize they should have prepared their gear earlier, delaying their first attempt at casting into the holes between the rocks for almost half an hour.

After several attempts to rewind the monofilament and change the bait, they finally succeed in each catching a few bluefin trevally weighing between 3 and 5 kilograms. They are happy not to return empty-handed. A light rain shower forces them to stop at the Jissang store. Joseph buys some cold Heineken cans while waiting for the weather to clear up. As they resume their motorcycle ride on the road in Papenoo, they see an immense rainbow touching the horizon.

Chapter 30

One Ruv

Takashi left for Japan accompanied by his wife Anna. Joseph received a postcard after several weeks announcing that his wife was pregnant, and he sent them a congratulations card on behalf of all the hotel staff. He met Shohei, a new Japanese guide for the travel agency in Papeete. Shohei was also charming and well-informed about the agency's clients. One day, while he was at the reception for a group, he mentioned to Joseph, indicating that he would take care of one of the women who came with the group, leaving the other to Joseph.

Their encounter took place at the Mahana Bar of the hotel with the two women, "O.L.". Suddenly, Shohei stood up, offering to take the woman named Ayako with him by car. In this unexpected moment, Joseph suggested to Noriko to follow him for a ride on his motorcycle. They rode early in the evening to Papeete, and Joseph stopped in front of the Lou Pescadou restaurant, an Italian restaurant on Cardella Street. They ordered a seafood pizza and a bottle of Sauvignon Blanc. Noriko was delighted, admitting that it was the first time she had ridden a motorcycle. The restaurant was lively with Mario, the chef, singing classic Italian songs while preparing pizzas in the wood-fired oven. They enjoyed the Italian flavors and ordered coffee, sharing a lemon tart. They returned through the side streets and the winding roads, Noriko holding Joseph with her delicate fair hands.

After parking his motorcycle inside the gate to the back office, Joseph suggested a walk in the park in front of the entrance of the Tahara'a, where a path led them to the cliffside viewpoint. The large trunks of the Aito(Ironwood) trees, imposing like Roman columns, sheltered this enchanting space with well-placed benches to relax and enjoy the panoramic historic site. The view of Matavai Bay illuminated by the full moon and a few lights from the houses along the shoreline made Noriko squeeze Joseph's arm tightly. Grateful for the evening, she invited him to accompany her to her room. Opening the door with her key, she embraced Joseph. Noriko would spend the entire vacation week with Joseph.

The days spent together, marked by intimate memories, seemed to pass all too quickly for the both of them. They promised to stay in touch, as Noriko had some notions of writing in English. For Joseph, his friend's absence left a void, but he understood that for her, it was an escape from her daily life at the office, as an employee in a large factory of a cosmetics company. However, in hindsight, Joseph realized that he did not feel the same sentiment, the memories with Noriko not equaling his great love in Hawaii with his dear Seo-Yeon.

Listening to Mendelssohn's violin concerto, enveloped by the music, Joseph felt inspiration rising within him. He took his fountain pen and began writing a letter to Seo Yeon and Hana. With a hint of concern over their silence in recent months, he nonetheless expressed his wishes for peace and happiness in their daily lives in Seoul. He shared with them the splendors of his vacation in Bora Bora, evoking the shimmering hues of the lagoon and the richness of marine life, as well as the warm welcome of the island's inhabitants. He also mentioned his request for a transfer to the hotel in Bora Bora, eagerly awaiting news on that front.

Joseph receives Hana's letter with sincere joy, expressing their happiness at maintaining contact. He is delighted to learn that Seo-Yeon and Hana are experiencing great success as a musical duo, performing at wedding receptions and charity events in various cities across South Korea, such as Incheon, Busan, and Daegu. Their bustling life leads them to stay in grand hotels across the country. As for Mi-cha, she embarked on a trip to New York to meet Steven's family, offering an international perspective to their circle of friends. These news warm Joseph's heart, reminding him of the importance of the bonds they have forged despite the distance.

Chapter 31

Transfer

The embarrassing situation faced by the management of Bora Bora and Samantha led to an important decision. Despite the expectations associated with her Japanese last name, Samantha did not speak Japanese, which caused difficulties when a group of demanding Japanese clients arrived. This situation resulted in a reorganization of the staff, with Joseph being transferred to Bora Bora while Samantha would return to Tahiti to work at the Reservations department of the Hotel Tahara'a. These news marked a turning point in Joseph's life, as he had been waiting for this opportunity for almost a year, thus marking the beginning of a new chapter for him.

Joseph's first job in Bora Bora was in the accounting department, where he worked as a night auditor. His shifts extended from 10:00 PM to 6:00 AM, during which he handled the check-outs of early morning departing guests. His job involved meticulously checking the accounting books, the day's revenues, and consolidating the accounts into a nightly report. This demanding task required great vigilance, especially since Joseph had to find sleep during the day, posing a real challenge to maintaining his effectiveness at work.

To streamline his work, Joseph adopted a proactive approach by often arriving at the workplace well before the scheduled time. He reviewed the various revenues of the day, stemming from receipts from the shop, the restaurant, the beach bar, the main bar, and client excursions. All of this had to be recorded by hand, with the check-out bills for departing clients needing to be typed up for a neat presentation using carbon paper to make copies. Additionally, he had to keep track of the accounts of local clients who frequented the establishment regularly. Immersed in the silence of the night, Joseph focused on the details of accounting, only breaking the silence to exchange a few words with the night watchman making rounds to ensure the property's security. Come morning, after completing his work, he returned home exhausted, allowing himself a few hours of sleep before being awakened by the sounds of the upcoming day. This demanding routine underscored Joseph's discipline and dedication to his work, despite the inherent challenges of the nocturnal work schedule.

While waiting for the summaries and receipts from the restaurants and bars, Joseph would meet with the various cashiers who had finished their shifts. They brought their cash floats, consisting of Polynesian bills and coins, and Joseph had to meticulously audit each cash register. During this process, one of the cashiers named Delphine would notice him and playfully tease him while handing over her cash and documents. Joseph, engrossed in his work, only had time to offer her a smile in response.

In addition to his essential responsibilities, Joseph was often called upon to welcome Japanese guests during the day. Amidst his fragmented moments of rest, he had to ensure that the Japanese guests had an enjoyable stay in Bora Bora. However, after a few months, his body had adjusted to the chaotic rhythm of his life, finally allowing him some time for leisure. Craig, the director of purchasing, owned a boat moored on the shore, and he invited Joseph for a fishing trip aboard, teaching him the basics of trolling. Their vessel, a small 17-foot boat, allowed them to fish inside the lagoon. Barely had they put their lines behind the boat when beautiful bluefin trevally were hooked.

Chapter 32

The Reef

Craig also wished to share a secret with Joseph. Around five in the morning, before daybreak, in the peaceful darkness on the hotel's boat dock, nestled between the overwater bungalows, he showed Joseph the art of casting. The technique involved switching the reel to silent mode, and then swiftly reeling in the nylon, making the lure dance like a wounded little fish, thus provoking the attacks of the trevally. In the morning silence, they walked along the pier with their fishing rods, skillfully casting their lures. Joseph was amazed at how many fish they could catch with each attempt. After catching a dozen fish between them, they returned, admiring their morning haul in the emerging light of day.

One morning, as the fish seemed to be avoiding the dock, Craig decided to take Joseph for a walk through the gardens, leading them to the point between the two beaches of the property. On the very first cast, Joseph hooked a trevally weighing about 8 kilograms. Craig also managed to catch one of similar size. As they made their way towards Matira, at every new spot they tried their luck, they caught beautiful bluefin trevally as well as white trevally with a golden stripe. For Joseph, it was much more than just fishing; it was a rediscovery of the passion his father had tried to instill in him long ago.

Craig took Joseph out early in the morning on his boat towards the coral reef that separated the lagoon from the ocean. Gliding through the turquoise lagoon on his small 17-foot boat equipped with a 30-horsepower outboard motor, they were surrounded by dark corals that marked the landscape. Suddenly, the water color shifted from a deep blue to a lighter, clearer hue, indicating a dramatic change in depth. Below, the white sand reflected the sky, and a few seabirds soared above, seeking their prey among the small fish. As they slowed the boat down, two leopard rays gracefully glided past the coral. Anchoring the boat next to a volcanic rock formation, the two fishermen began to wade among the coral, avoiding the black-blue sea urchins with their formidable spines. The waves relentlessly crashed onto the reef, creating a striking panorama of the ocean, the reef, and the vast sky as far as the eye could see. Climbing onto the reef, Joseph felt on the edge of existence, enveloped by the majesty of nature.

This style of fishing required spotting the crevices in the reef formation to be able to cast the lures into the heart of this space. Amidst the ebb and flow of the current brought by the waves, Joseph patiently awaited the right moment, scrutinizing every movement of the water. When calm returned after the water receded, he seized the opportunity and cast his lure, hoping for a fruitful catch. However, his first attempt was interrupted by a brief but intense struggle with a big fish, which ended in the breaking of the leader on the rocks within the crevice. Despite his repeated efforts, Joseph failed to catch any fish, while Craig returned with a beautiful 6-kilo trevally. Disappointed, Joseph noticed an octopus in the shallow waters. Ready to hook it with his small gaff, he suddenly realized that the creature had only three legs. Touched by this discovery, he decided to let the octopus return to its refuge in its hideaway, filled with compassion for this nature-disabled creature.

The effect of the morning sun wasn't immediately apparent during their reef exploration. However, that evening before going to work, Joseph saw his reflection in the mirror and discovered a terrible sunburn. Red and black spots adorned his skin, already beginning to peel. He felt pain everywhere: on his forehead and his face, neck, arms and legs, as if he had been exposed to a fire. Since that experience,

Joseph would take care to protect himself with sunscreen even during his bike rides, aware of the danger of the sun's rays.

Chapter 33

Presto Resto

Going out with new colleagues like Craig made Joseph realize the lack of interaction with other staff members and clients. Despite the long hours spent in the silence of his accounting work, he felt a void. One day, he clashed with the accountant, who accused him of not searching hard enough for the right numbers to balance the books. Frustrated, he requested a meeting with the manager and expressed his desire to leave the accounting department as soon as possible. Understanding his situation, the manager, who had also struggled with the uncommunicative Chinese accountant, offered him the position of restaurant manager. For Joseph, it was a positive change, especially since he had kept an admiring eye on Delphine, who worked at the beach bar.

At first, Joseph found it challenging to adjust to the restaurant's working hours, especially to cover the breakfast and dinner shifts. Fortunately, the restaurant was often quiet during lunchtime, as guests preferred to dine at the beach bar or go on excursions. This often gave him breaks in the afternoon, which he used to go cycling around the island. He met a former rider, Teamo from the Orohena cycling club, who had returned to Bora Bora with his family. Together, they explored doing laps around a 5k stretch at a good pace. These moments of relaxation on two wheels allowed him to recharge and appreciate the beauty of the island in a different way.

It was a new challenge for Joseph to become the official photographer for the hotel's employee ID photos, a task he approached with seriousness despite his lack of experience compared to his brother Michael. With the photographic equipment inherited from his brother, he embarked on this new responsibility with determination. He set up a small darkroom in the bungalow to develop black and white film. Another opportunity arose when the manager asked him to capture special moments involving celebrities staying at the hotel, to be featured in the Dépêche de Tahiti, the daily newspaper published in Papeete. It was an unexpected chance for Joseph to hone his photographic skills while contributing to the hotel's visibility in the local media.

Joseph also had the delicate task of welcoming and guiding Japanese guests at the restaurant, ensuring smooth service. When explaining the concept of the breakfast buffet to tour guides, he often noticed their amused reaction when they used the word "Baikin," which means "bacteria" in Japanese. Joseph refrained from laughing out loud, knowing that the guides were referring to the famous buffet at the "the Viking" restaurant at the Imperial Hotel in Tokyo. It was a light-hearted anecdote that highlighted the linguistic and cultural nuances he had to navigate in his role as a host.

Chapter 34

Nocturnal reef

On weekends, the nightclub Le Récif was a unique spot for the local crowd, for entertainment with loud music and the bar was constantly busy and crowded. By 10 p.m., the street filled with scooters, motorcycles, and a few cars, their occupants preparing to enter the establishment or others exiting to take a break or meet friends. Craig had invited Joseph to join him, offering a ride from the hotel in his Mini Moke. In the disco atmosphere, with the sparkling globe hanging from the ceiling, Joseph sipped his beer and spotted Delphine at the end of the bar with talking to her friends. She invited him to dance, swept away by the deafening music, her infectious smile transcending the sound barrier.

Joseph felt a bit awkward, not being used to dancing, but he admired Delphine's natural movements. After a few lively songs, the music changed to a slow dance, and Delphine didn't let Joseph go, taking him in her arms. He accepted the invitation, expressing their mutual admiration as he noticed the Tiare flowers that adorned her hair. After a series of dances, Joseph sat on a bench to rest, watching the other dancers as they continued to move to the music. After drinking a few more beers, Joseph began to feel the effects of the alcohol and decided it was time to leave. He looked for Craig, but could not find him. He then realized that Delphine had already advised Craig that she would take him back on her scooter.

Holding onto Delphine's waist, Joseph gazed at the road illuminated by the full moon and the scooter's headlight. The silhouettes of coconut trees and the reflections of the lagoon danced to the rhythm of the vehicle. They found their way to the small pandanus "fare poté," used as a garage for scooters and motorcycles. Together, they climbed the path to the entrance of the bungalow. Although he hadn't wished for things to escalate so quickly, Joseph was grateful to see that Delphine seemed to share the same approach, simply desiring rest and nothing more. As he let her sleep, he felt a deep mutual respect and was thankful to return home safe and sound.

The next day at work, Craig teased Joseph upon noticing women's shoes outside his door. Joseph responded with a smile and thanked him for their evening at Le Récif. Craig would regularly invite Joseph for a beer or sometimes dinner at his home with his Tahitian wife. During the next dinner, Erina, Craig's wife, cheerfully asked, "When is the wedding?" This warm and friendly atmosphere finally made Joseph feel a sense of happiness in his work, giving him much greater ease than at the beginning.

Chapter 35

Realization

After three years in French Polynesia, a tropical opportunity presented itself to Joseph, but he decided to stay true to his aspirations. His desire to work for an international company persisted, as it would allow him to travel and explore various countries and their cultures. However, an unexpected strike by hotel employees led to the closure of the establishment for two months. During this period of closure and "ristora" or restructuring of staff, management decided to proceed with renovations on the bungalows and in the property's gardens. With his accumulated leave, Joseph seized the opportunity to organize a trip back to Hawaii to visit his family.

During his days at the Manoa home, Joseph relished the delights of Japanese cuisine and shared a few restaurant outings with his parents and Susanne. His sister continued her studies in music but had just returned from Japan after spending a year studying Japanese culture. She even considered pursuing a Ph.D. in Japanese history. Meanwhile, Joseph learned that Michael and his wife had moved into a new home in New Jersey. With a degree in Japanese, Michael was a teacher at the prestigious Seton Hall University on the American mainland. During a family meal at the Maple Garden Chinese restaurant, the idea of visiting his brother sparked in Joseph's mind, and his mother immediately expressed her desire to accompany him on this journey.

Michael and his Japanese wife, Seiko, were delighted to reunite with the two small travelers amidst the bustling crowd of New Yorkers upon their arrival at JFK airport. As they crossed the New Jersey

Turnpike, Joseph was amazed by the impressive number of cars on the suspension bridge. To celebrate their reunion, Michael had prepared a feast with his wife, blending Japanese flavors with American ingredients, including delicious sashimi of striped bass.

At Michael's apartment, there was a designated office space adorned with numerous books in both Japanese and English, along with a large tape recorder equipped with a microphone and a pair of headphones in one corner. Joseph learned that Michael was involved in a simultaneous interpretation project with his professor at Seton Hall.

During dinner, Michael suggested taking Joseph to the cinema to see the latest movie, 'Apocalypse Now'. At the Ziegfeld Theatre in the capital, Joseph felt as though The Doors were playing live behind the curtains at the start of the film. The movie deeply resonated with the two brothers, recalling the dark period of the Vietnam War that had even affected their peaceful life in Hawaii. Michael had lost high school friends in this conflict and had visited their graves with other colleagues. On his part, Joseph had been fortunate to avoid active military service due to his above average grades in high school, allowing him to bypass the American conscription system, known as the "draft." This system had evolved into a lottery based on birthdate, and the numbers assigned to Joseph and Michael had spared them from immediate conscription. Nevertheless, the threat of being sent to war loomed over many young men, and the film stirred up these unsettling memories for both of them.

While Michael was at the university, Joseph and his mother explored the Metropolitan Museum. As they admired the paintings of European masters, Joseph's mother was surprised and proud of the knowledge Joseph demonstrated, gained from his experiences in Europe. Yet, he couldn't help but think of his friends Lawrence and Anton, the two art enthusiasts who had taught him so much. After a lunch break at a nearby restaurant, Michael picked them up in his car. In a neighborhood of the Big Apple, he took them to a few clothing and souvenir shops, as well as a music instrument store. Michael had kept his passion for the guitar and became interested in one in particular at this store. It was a Gibson from the 1950s, an electric guitar found in a closet tucked away in a corner of the city, and the seller seemed perplexed, unable to find a price for this gem. Michael bought it for $300 and grinned in the car, saying it might be worth more than $4000!

The next day, Michael took Joseph into the city, encouraging him to apply for a position at the United Nations. As they walked through the bustling capital among the well-dressed crowd in business attire, Joseph observed the flags fluttering in the wind, aligned in front of the famous United Nations building. Thanks to Michael's Seton Hall faculty ID, they were able to access the reception area where Joseph received a job application. Upon leaving, Michael emphasized that it was a great opportunity, highlighting his brother's linguistic skills, as Joseph spoke three languages. Joseph took his words into consideration, but he realized he could not even see the top of the famous building, perhaps symbolizing a greater challenge than anticipated. Back at Michael's place, Joseph called his sempai Lionel, who had become the resident manager at the Hotel Tahara'a. He asked if there was still a possibility of returning to his Polynesian family.

For their final weekend together, the small family headed north to upstate New York to visit an apple orchard. It was a magical moment characterized by the "Indian Summer," a period when temperatures rise after autumn, offering a calm before winter. On the orchard, they discovered different apple varieties, and each visitor could fill a bag with as many apples as they wished. For Joseph, this experience reignited nostalgic memories of his days at Safeway, where he used to stock apples, often juggling three of them in one hand. He could recognize the varieties on the orchard with a sense of familiarity.

These enjoyable moments with his mother, Michael, and Seiko reminded Joseph of his passion for his collection of classical music LPs, especially when he listened to Vivaldi's "Four Seasons" violin concerto. Such moments made him realize the changing beauty of the seasons, a sensation foreign to him since his arrival in Tahiti, where only one season of sunshine prevails, with its turquoise waters bordered by the coral reef and the Pacific Ocean. In his mind and in his heart, Joseph is already transported to this island where he finds a harmonious balance with the surrounding nature.

As he loaded their suitcases into the car trunk, Joseph noticed a sleeping tri-colored cat near a weeping willow next to the parking lot. It had found a sunny spot for "hinata bocco" (sunbathing nap), offering a peaceful and serene sight. This scene took Joseph back to his youth, reminiscing about their big dog, King, a speckled white English setter, dozing in in their garden in Akasaka. It was a simple yet nostalgic moment, reminding him of his grandmother and the simplicity and tranquility of life. Returning home, Joseph yearned to rediscover that same peace, away from the hustle and bustle of big metropolitan cities. Like the animals peacefully sleeping, he hoped to find his own haven where he could recharge and rest.

Chapter 36

Urashima Taro

The reunion with the staff at Hotel Tahara'a, under Lionel's direction, was heartwarming for Joseph, who felt like he was back among his extended family. Raising their glasses at the Mahana Bar, Joseph and his friends toasted in a friendly atmosphere, while he gazed at the magnificent Matavai Bay, with Moorea Island in the background. The cloud-covered mountains, the endless ocean, and the vast blue sky offered a comforting familiar sight. With a few months of work in Tahiti before heading back to Bora Bora, Joseph arranged to have his bike shipped via maritime freight on the Taporo ship, which supplied the Leeward Islands once a week. This prospect allowed him to look forward to rediscovering the joys of cycling amidst the breathtaking landscapes of French Polynesia.

As Joseph cycles the roads of Mahina and Papenoo, he appreciates the sight of lush valleys and distant mountains. Crossing the bridge over the stream, he notices a woman on her scooter heading in the opposite direction. In Papenoo, he observes the surfers, their cars lined up along the road, eagerly awaiting the perfect wave. On the straight stretch, he takes in the vastness of the Pacific Ocean and the waves crashing against the rocks. The cries of birds and the gentle breeze add to the heavenly ambiance of Tahiti's east coast. Riding past the "trou de souffleur,"(blow hole) Joseph goes up the short hill and feels the first drops a divine shower as he ascends. Upon turning around, he watches the bay fade into darkness, but as he continues to pedal around the shoreline, the gray sky clears to reveal a massive rainbow spanning across the misty rain. Joseph is filled with happiness at having rediscovered his tropical paradise.

The return to Bora Bora for Joseph was marked by an unexpected reality: a low hotel occupancy rate, resulting from its recent closure and ongoing renovations. The resignation of Chris, the Rooms Division Manager after five years of service, added another dimension to this transition period. Faced with this situation, Monty the director offered Joseph the position, entrusting him with new responsibilities as head of guest services and receptionists, as well as coordinating with the reservations office. This change posed a challenge for Joseph, but he was determined to succeed, guided by Chris's teachings and ready to confront the challenges ahead with confidence.

Meanwhile, one of the hotel's concessionaires, Erwin, who had founded Moana Adventure Tours, would become a good friend to Joseph. He offered various water excursions to guests, including water skiing, scuba diving, glass-bottom boat tours, and other activities in the lagoon, such as coastal fishing. Erwin offered Joseph an initiation dive for scuba diving, but Joseph hesitated, recalling his near-drowning experiences in Tahiti. However, encouraged by Erwin and grateful for his kindness and constant support, Joseph overcame his initial apprehension. Erwin was surprised to see how well Joseph controlled his breathing during the initiation and encouraged him to pursue diving lessons. Putting aside his fears, Joseph persevered and eventually obtained his FFESSM level one diving certificate, achieving a new milestone in his journey in Bora Bora.

Discovering the silent world between 15 and 20 meters deep, Joseph was mesmerized by what he saw. He felt connected to the ocean panorama, dazzled by the explosion of colors from the various coral formations and the diversity of fish. In some valleys, eagle rays, a large family of about twenty individuals, offered a ballet in harmony with the current. Other majestic creatures, like manta rays gracefully crossing the lagoon, as well as a large turtle measuring nearly a meter, glided gracefully through the waters. As he watched in awe, two large bluefin trevally passed just inches from him, offering him incredible proximity to these magnificent marine creatures. Joseph thus became a passionate new observer of the underwater world. Before diving outside the reef, as they prepared on the boat, Joseph and his dive instructor, Taaroa, were fortunate to notice a whale leap from the surface only 300 meters from the boat. During their dive, they were accompanied by the strident "conversation"of a female whale and her calf, an extraordinary experience that would remain etched in their memories. And despite the presence of reef sharks circling their territory, Joseph felt in harmony with this fascinating ecosystem, knowing they posed no danger to them.

The legend of Urashima Taro resonated deeply in Joseph's mind as he walked along the beach. This fairy tale, inherited from his grandmother, was steeped in wisdom and mystery. Taro, the hero from the distant island, had experienced an extraordinary adventure, saving a mistreated turtle and being rewarded with a visit to the underwater palace by the turtle's father. Upon returning to the beach after a few days, he discovered that the entire village had vanished and a century had passed.

As he pondered this fairy tale, Joseph couldn't help but reflect on his own life, his relationships, and the fear of losing everything one day. Like Taro, he had felt the grandeur of the unknown, the fragile beauty of life, and the fear of impermanence. But just as Taro had been guided by his heart and courage, Joseph felt inspired to embrace each moment, each relationship, with gratitude and love, knowing that life is as changeable as the tides of the ocean.

As he contemplates the serene landscape around him, Joseph recalls a few words from Baudelaire. Traveling through crystalline waters and white sandy beaches, he wonders if he had perhaps already achieved a certain luxury, calm, and voluptuousness. For him, luxury is not found in material possessions, but in experiences rich with wonder and connection to nature. Calm, on the other hand, is found in moments of inner peace, far from the tumult of the modern world. Voluptuousness is discovered in the simple pleasures of life, in warm encounters and moments of shared joy. Through his travels and encounters, Joseph realizes that these words are states of mind more than physical destinations. It is in the contemplation of the beauty surrounding him, in gratitude for precious moments, and in the love shared with those around him that he truly finds the richness of life.

Part 2
Chapter 1

Bora Bora Paradise

Working as a Front Office Manager in Tahiti certainly had prepared Joseph for his current role in Bora Bora. His familiarity with daily tasks and previous contacts with tour guides allowed him to integrate quickly into his new position. With occupancy rates on the rise, Joseph now finds himself busy from morning till night, juggling the increasing responsibilities of his role. Being called upon once a week to take on the role of Duty Manager is a testament to the management's confidence in his abilities and his capacity to effectively handle hotel operations, even in demanding and time-critical situations.

Joseph's relationship with Delphine has evolved into cohabitation, a commitment that has been greeted with friendly teasing from his colleagues. Their mutual connection ran deep, based on honesty and simplicity, qualities that made Joseph a cherished partner in Delphine's eyes. Although their intimacy took time to develop, their emotional bond strengthened through shared anecdotes and discoveries of Polynesian culture. Meeting Delphine's daughter, Noelani, was an emotional moment for Joseph, who instantly felt a familial connection with this charming child, already considering her as his own daughter.

Leaving the bicycle aside, Joseph and Delphine explored the island riding on a Yamaha 175 motorcycle. The trails led them uphill, to the radio antenna located on the southern tip of the island. From up there, they could contemplate the breathtaking panorama of the turquoise lagoon, with its changing shades indicating depth, and the sparkling white sand under the blue sky. The coral reef was clearly outlined, separating the deep blue ocean from the clearer waters of the lagoon. The relentless waves crashed onto the reef, creating a mesmerizing spectacle. The roofs of the hotel bungalows seemed tiny from this elevated vantage point, and they even spotted a scooter slowly passing on the island road.

The small post office, the bank, Chin Lee's store, and a few small shops scattered around the island bore witness to the simple and peaceful life that prevailed in Bora Bora. In the hotel bungalows, the absence of telephones was notable, as was the case in the office. A radio booth served as a means of communication with Hotel Tahara'a. Communications were conducted by pressing a button to speak and releasing it to listen to responses or requests from Tahiti. Lionel, the director, had established a centralized reservation system at the Hotel Tahara'a which would benefit Hotel Bora Bora by attracting new clients, resulting in an increase in occupancy rates. Monty, the manager was often in the booth to discuss matters with Lionel. In case of a need for maintenance equipment, Chief Engineer Dave communicated with Purchasing Manager Jeff via the booth. Craig was also a regular in the booth, and once the day's communications were over, Joseph sometimes received a friendly call from Lionel.

Chapter 2

Fountain pen

Communication between Joseph and the Korean sisters was gradually slowing down, limited to an annual letter and New Year's cards at the beginning of each year. Seo Yeon and Hana continued their classical duo career, occasionally performing at charity events in Singapore, Taipei, Hong Kong, and Tokyo. They were delighted to explore other countries and their unique cultures and cuisines. Hana maintained a form of honorific politeness in her writings, accompanying her letters with some photos of their performances. Their mother had been placed in a nursing home, while they continued to reside in the family home in Seoul, their father having found an apartment downtown. Joseph was pleased to learn that Mi-cha had given birth to twin girls and had settled into a large house with Steven in New York. He responded by warmly congratulating them, promising to send a small gift for the twins. He also shared details about his life in Bora Bora, mentioning his newfound friendship with Delphine and his commitment to his work, which was keeping him in Polynesia.

He received updates from Takashi, and his responsibilities as a "sarari-man" or working individual in a big corporation. They would raise their daughter Naomi in Tokyo. Joseph responded to Takashi, offering him congratulations and encouragement. He chose not to delve into the details of his own romantic relationships, instead focusing on discussing his adaptation to life on the paradise island and his new activities, such as diving and fishing.

Two months later, Joseph received a letter from Mi-cha along with some family photos featuring the twins. She expressed warm gratitude to Joseph for the adorable Polynesian clothes and toys that Delphine had added to the package. Mi-cha mentioned that she had stopped working to fully dedicate herself to raising her children, who would grow up in America. This news reassured Joseph, knowing that Delphine had not reacted jealously to the attention he paid to Mi-cha's family. By sharing his own romantic past in Hawaii with Delphine, she had understood Joseph's deep compassion. Grateful for the peace of mind this mutual understanding brought him, Joseph took his fountain pen and sent a postcard from Bora Bora to New York, expressing his gratitude for the precious bonds he maintained with his family and loved ones, even thousands of miles away.

Joseph had noticed the turtle logo on the postcards he sent, a familiar symbol he had seen before on Erwin's boats from Moana Adventure Tours. During their next meeting at the reception, Joseph discovered that his friend was actually a professional photographer, having collaborated on a reference book titled "Fishes of Polynesia" and another pictorial book, "Bora Bora". He also had other book projects. When Joseph expressed his admiration for his work, Erwin generously gifted him with a dozen photography magazines and some books the next day. Joseph's encounter with Erwin opened new horions, inspiring him to explore the world of photography further and consider new ways to capture the beauty and diversity of Polynesia through his lens.

Listening to Mendelssohn, immersed in the music, Joseph was engulfed by a wave of memories and reflections. The Korean sisters, with their lives in Seoul and New York, evoked both nostalgia and joy for their respective journeys. The news of Mi-cha's children reminded him of an anecdote shared by his brother Michael during his stay. Professor Park, a Korean who led the simultaneous interpretation project, had a son facing difficulties in the American school due to a language barrier. He initiated a movement for a bilingual program in schools with a significant percentage of foreign students. This initiative led to the acceptance of a bilingual education system in American schools. Inspired by this story, Joseph took his fountain pen to write to Mi-cha, expressing his wishes of kindness for her twins and a future filled with hope. This showcased the importance of cultural diversity and the preservation of languages and traditions, values dear to Joseph and deeply resonating with his experience and attachment to Polynesia and his own roots.

Chapter 3

Samurai Tinito

Riding around the island on his bike, Joseph was often greeted by locals along the roadside, with words like "Iaorana Tinito"(Hello Chinaman). In Tahiti and the surrounding islands, the Chinese community was already well-established, creating an atmosphere of diversity alongside the Polynesians. Joseph appreciated this recognition as a foreigner while feeling fully accepted by all. Continuing his quest for knowledge, Joseph devoured the magazines and books left by hotel guests. In one of these readings, he discovered the origin of the word "Iaorana," the Polynesian greeting rooted in the interaction between English missionaries and the people of Tahiti in the late 18th century. The anecdote about Polynesian children learning English, with greetings like "Good Morning your Honor," which eventually transformed into "Iaorana," provided a fascinating insight into the linguistic and cultural evolution of the region.

Welcoming Japanese guests at the hotel, the staff quickly noticed that Joseph wasn't quite Chinese Due to their interest in Japanese culture and martial arts, he was nicknamed "Samurai" by colleagues. Since childhood, Joseph had been captivated by "chanbara" or samurai films. He passionately read the works of Eiji Yoshikawa about the famous warrior Miyamoto Musashi. This immersion in Japanese culture had offered him a fascinating insight into the philosophy and traditions of his home country.

While riding the motorcycle one evening with Delphine, they stopped at the Vaitape pier. The distant reef waves could be heard, and

Joseph noticed some splashes on the surface of the darkened lagoon. There was a gentle current and a trade wind causing Delphine's shoulder length hair to dance around her neck. She mentioned that they were "aturés" or small mackerels and Joseph remembered the same name in Hawaiian, "akule". They were attracted to shore in the evening to hunt for tiny fish prey. Knowing these fish were delicious, upon returning, Joseph prepared his small fishing rod with fine nylon on the reel and small lures. After three-quarters of an hour, they saw that they had filled a bucket with over twenty fish. Preparing to leave, they noticed an old Tahitian fisherman sitting on the pier with a long rod. His colleague had just arrived on a bicycle, carrying his fishing rod. He asked if they were biting. The old fisherman replied, "Aita"(no) not tonight, the tinito caught them all!"

In the beginning, Delphine watched Joseph catch the fish, and she was joyful upon returning home to prepare the catch of the day for everyone and Noelani loved to eat fish. Before their next outing to the pier, Joseph prepared a second fishing rod for the fishing session. It was a 1.5-meter short fiberglass rod with a small reel filled with fine monofilament, which he handed to Delphine, showing her how to handle the rod and reel. After a few tries, she also became an expert catching aturé. Joseph had a stiffer carbon fiber rod, and he managed to catch two "omuri" or big eyed trevally weighing 2 to 3 kilograms each. The two old fishermen on the pier couldn't believe their eyes, gaping in astonishment, their buckets remaining empty.

Chapter 4

Eia, Fée

Craig suggested to Joseph to invest in a motorized outrigger canoe, and he discussed it with a Polynesian carpenter who crafted fishing canoes in Amanahune, one of the villages on the island. With his salary, Joseph decided to embark on this venture. After a month and a half, the old Polynesian wood artisan had added layer of fiberglass and blue paint to the canoe. There was a "purera" (prayer) ceremony before Joseph could take possession of the canoe, in the presence of the artisan's entire family who surrounded the 17-foot vessel, placing "tiare tahiti"(tiny gardenia like white flowers) leis on its bow. Finally, Joseph could use the canoe at his leisure for fishing, having also acquired a second hand 15 horsepower Johnson outboard motor. At first, he kept the canoe next to Craig's, the manager's, and the assistant manager's boats, on the shore, at the end of the hotel's property.

Delphine still worked at the beach bar, alongside her aunt Tehi and the other young barmaids. With the turquoise lagoon as a backdrop, customers could enjoy refreshing drinks and order simple dishes. The kitchen, located in the main building, was accessible by a staircase made of various pieces of cemented stone. The atmosphere was friendly and often light-hearted as they communicated with the central kitchen to place orders for customers using the two way radio. A mixture of English, Tahitian, and French punctuated their exchanges, for example: "Hoe(one) Cheeseburger, avec frites(French fries), Hoe Mahi Burger avec salad, au lieu de frites," to which the kitchen would respond: "Hoe Cheese, Hoe Mahi avec salad, OK OK" Within fifteen minutes,

Delphine or one of the other barmaids would walk up to the kitchen and return with the dishes laden on a large tray, with several customers' orders.

When Delphine and Joseph both had their days off together, they would embark on the motorized canoe to explore the different corners of the lagoon, whether for trolling or leaving the canoe on a beach. On one of the "motus" (islets), while Delphine succeeded in catching "tarao" or "roi" (small groupers), Joseph donned a mask, snorkel, and fins to search for fée (octopus) in the crystal-clear waters of the lagoon. With a Hawaiian sling, he managed to capture an octopus, which he placed in a bucket aboard the canoe. He prepared his fishing rod and used a small piece of octopus as bait. Barely had he cast his bait into the water when he felt a violent tug on his line. For nearly ten minutes, he maneuvered the rod and reel and finally managed to catch a bluefin trevally of about 7 kilograms from the deeper part of the lagoon.

To facilitate fishing, Delphine had cut some long strips of purau(tree) bark. She showed Joseph how to tie the strip around his waist like a belt, and as they caught a fish, they would thread each fish through, passing the bark between the gills, then sliding the fish all the way down, secured by a piece of floating wood. This became a "tuii"(stringer) of "eia" (fresh fish). The float was important to avoid attacks from moray eels. Delphine also pointed out that the purau flowers, a type of wild hibiscus, changed color. In the morning, the flower was yellow, in the afternoon it turned orange, and by evening, falling to the ground, the same flower became red. Nature's pendulum marked the passage of time in paradise.

Joseph called to Delphine with a gesture, indicating it was time to head back, as they had plenty to feast on with their catches, his "tuii" becoming heavy. Back on the canoe, they were fortunate to spot a few dolphins leaping in front of their small vessel, navigating the deep waters of the Teavanui channel. As they approached the main island, Joseph observed a man riding a bicycle slowly along the shore, passing by modest plywood houses in vibrant colors, topped with tin roofs, and a "faré poté" (pavilion) with a pandanus roof. Delphine's family resided in the heart of Faanui Bay. After anchoring the canoe in shallow waters, Delphine's father, Tihani, came to help them unload. Upon arriving at the house, they were warmly welcomed by the cheerful voice of little Noelani and by mother Rota, who marveled at the fresh fish and octopus. Joseph was surprised to see the father carrying the outboard motor on his shoulder for safety reasons. He found a small shelter under the mango tree in the garden to store the motor. From that day on, the canoe would remain in the lagoon in front of Delphine's house in Faanui, bringing the simple joy of providing fish to the family and sharing these moments with everyone.

Chapter 5

Friends

Since its opening in 1961, the Hotel Bora Bora welcomed loyal clientele who returned year after year. This tradition continued as Joseph managed the reception, diligently noting down reservations. Despite the absence of computers, management was handled with reservation charts with grids, pencils to fill in for each reservation, with the ability to erase for modifications. However, overbookings, especially for the limited number of overwater bungalows, of which there were only fifteen, could pose delicate issues. In such situations, Joseph had to appease the guests by assigning them other beach bungalows, accompanied by some gifts from the management. Fortunately, most guests quickly forgot the inconveniences, prioritizing the overall experience offered by the hotel.

In the case of the Japanese honeymooners, the Yamamotos, faced with the unavailability of the overwater bungalow reserved for the first two days of their stay, Joseph took steps to mitigate their disappointment. He tasked Carmen, a receptionist, with welcoming the Yamamotos at the Bora Bora airport with a warm smile, despite the language barrier. Carmen became their point of contact during their stay, charming the Japanese with her authentic Polynesian hospitality. Joseph humbly apologized on behalf of the management, acknowledging the importance of their honeymoon trip. The Yamamotos were pleasantly surprised by the natural beauty and tranquility of the island, far from the hustle and bustle of Tokyo. They expressed their gratitude to Joseph and Carmen for their beachside stay, becoming loyal customers in the process. Over time, their relationship evolved from that of customers to dear friends of Joseph and Delphine, strengthening the bonds between the hotel and its loyal guests.

At the reception, Joseph noticed a Japanese man discreetly holding a cylindrical case while filling out his registration details. Curious, Joseph asked if he was bringing a fishing rod. With a broad smile, the man replied that he had just acquired a quality fishing rod but hadn't had the opportunity to use it in Japan. Aware of the hotel rules, Joseph reminded him that it was prohibited to fish between the bungalows or in front of the property. Shota, understanding the situation, asked if there were other places where he could fish. Joseph offered to accompany him early the next morning to show him a suitable spot where he had previously caught some nice fish.

In the early morning as the sun was coming up, they walked in silence on the sand of Matira Beach. Joseph showed him the "hole" or the area where the dark blue water reached close to the shoreline, indicating a sudden drop off. After several attempts, Shota succeeded in catching a beautiful 3-kilo bluefin trevally and a 2-kilo white trevally with a golden hue. Joseph advised him to bring the fish to the hotel kitchen to have them prepared. Thanks to this experience, Shota and his wife Mayumi became regular guests, enriching the relationship between the hotel and its loyal visitors.

Kevin and Vicki were loyal patrons from San Francisco, making a pilgrimage every year to discover Polynesian culture and enjoy the enchanting island of Bora Bora. With their friendly attitude, they were well-known to the hotel staff, learning even to speak the Polynesian language. During one of their visits, Kevin expressed a desire to meet the mayor of Bora Bora to discuss the island's history. As a lawyer, he wanted to explore the archives and libraries to uncover the truth about Bora Bora's past, convinced that no comprehensive book on the subject existed. Joseph, having forged close bonds, accompanied them to their meeting with "Tavana" or Mayor, acting as an interpreter. This encounter marked the beginning of a close friendship between Joseph and Kevin, who then set out to document the history of Bora Bora. Guided by his curiosity and desire for truth, Kevin embarked on a writing project to reveal the authentic history of this paradise island, far from the sometimes embellished narratives heard before.

Chapter 6

Heartbreak

The letter from Hana, coming from Singapore instead of the usual Seoul, brought surprise to Joseph. He noticed the words "Special Delivery" on the envelope. As he read it, he learned with sadness that during a recent performance at the Victoria Theatre in Singapore, Seo-Yeon had suffered a fainting spell, collapsing in front of the audience, causing shockwaves. Quickly attended to, she was rushed to Gleneagles Hospital, where doctors diagnosed her with a stroke. The situation plunged Hana into profound distress, keeping her awake all night by her friend's side in the hospital corridors.

In the morning, exhausted but resolved, Hana took the time to organize Seo Yeon's contact information and details of their medical coverage, at the hospital reception, while ensuring to maintain contact with Mi-Cha, mindful of the time difference so as not to disturb the twins' sleep. Returning to the hospital after a quick stop at the Regent Hotel to change, Hana was pleasantly surprised to find a bouquet of flowers from the hotel management, placed on a table at the I.C.U. near Seo Yeon's room. It was a comforting gesture that gave her some hope in this difficult time. She realized then that she was not alone in this ordeal, that friends and even strangers were there to support them. The kind presence of the doorman Alfred at the Regent Hotel, who had shown understanding and offered his support, had also touched Hana. These small gestures gave her the strength to face the days ahead as she remained by her sister's side, praying for her recovery.

Hana's letter, written with all the delicacy of honorifics, revealed the deep sorrow she felt. This new ordeal profoundly touched Joseph, strengthening the bond he shares with the Korean sisters' family, as he fervently hopes for Seo-Yeon's recovery. At the Bora Bora Post Office, Joseph took the time to send a telegram to Hana at the Hotel Regent in Singapore, expressing his sympathy and wishes for Seo Yeon's recovery. Every word was carefully chosen to convey his support in this difficult time. Back at the hotel, Joseph wasted no time in making a radio call to Lionel, asking him to coordinate the delivery of a floral arrangement to Gleneagles Hospital through the usual florist in downtown Papeete. These gestures, though modest, were filled with genuine sincerity, offering some comfort in the darkness of adversity.

In the heavy silence of their bungalow, Delphine sensed the weight of the sad news Joseph had just received. Her compassionate heart filled her with deep sorrow, and she held Joseph tightly, sharing his tears. It was then, in that moment of shared vulnerability, that Delphine chose to reveal news that, despite the difficult circumstances, would bring a ray of light: she was expecting a child. This announcement filled Joseph with indescribable emotion, mixing grief with joy, creating a whirlwind of feelings within him. In the ebb and flow of life's highs and lows, like the waves caressing the reef, Joseph found a refuge, a source of peace in this shared love and in the prospect of a new chapter to write together.

Chapter 7

Cyclonic

The devastating consequences of tropical cyclones struck the French Polynesia archipelago hard, amidst the El Niño phenomenon between 1982 and 1983. The island of Bora Bora suffered great damage during the Cyclone Rêva. Families were severely affected, losing their homes, roofs, and plantations. Fortunately, Delphine's house remained intact, although many trees and plants were uprooted.

On this stormy night, Joseph, Delphine, and their newborn son Eiji found refuge in the hotel manager's office, alongside other staff members and their families. However, the hotel itself was not spared, with several bungalows destroyed and others damaged, and the gardens littered with debris fallen branches, coconuts, and even uprooted trees. Fortunately, the guests had been evacuated to the island of Tahiti before the cyclone hit, ensuring their safety. This event was a stark reminder of the power of nature and the vulnerability of island communities to such extreme weather phenomena.

The scene after the cyclone was heartbreaking, with the coastal road blocked by fallen trees and debris, and visible damage to the houses. Delphine had to wait for two days before she could reunite with her family in Faanui. But as soon as she and Joseph were able to ride the motorcycle, with little Eiji snugly held against her, they quickly made their way to find the family, safe and sound.

In Faanui, Father Tihani and younger brother Armand were already clearing away debris, while Mother Rota, little Noelani, and

Delphine's sisters began preparing lunch. It was a moment of relief for Joseph to see that everyone was safe despite the damage caused by the cyclone. However, the news of the total destruction of his canoe added a dark note to this challenging time.

Joseph and Delphine were saddened and shocked as they toured around on the motorcycle. They witnessed several families forced to seek shelter under vinyl sheets turned into tents after losing their homes, with so many trees uprooted. However, despite this tragedy, each family seemed determined to rebuild, and sunny days brought renewed hope to all. The atmosphere of hope was also palpable at the hotel, where reconstruction work had already begun on the damaged bungalows and affected areas. Along the way, Joseph noticed a long fringing coral reef extending to the middle of the lagoon, likely created by a lava flow during the ancient formation of the island. He then envisioned returning one day to fish in this promising spot, located north of Faanui Bay.

Joseph's fishing trip in the Faanui lagoon proved fruitful despite the logistical challenges, now compelled to go there by motorcycle. Leaving the motorcycle by the purau tree, he cut a strip of bark to make his "tuii" or fish belt to string his catch. In the clear shallow water, he spots an octopus under a rock and manages to gaff it and put it in the yellow mesh bag. Balancing skillfully on the large rocks, he managed to reach deeper waters where he noticed birds hovering above the surface and some splashes. After two hours of effort, he started his Yamaha motorcycle to head home with a fine harvest of bluefin trevally and groupers and two octopus. On the way back, a memory brought a smile, as one of the types of groupers he caught, the "roi" with its dark brown color speckled with tiny blue spots, was the exact same color and pattern of the Pierre Cardin necktie his brother Michael had offered him as a birthday present. The other grouper called "tarao" has a lighter beige color with brown spots.

Upon his return home, enthusiasm filled the air, with the whole family preparing for the feast to come. Father Tihani contributed freshly opened coconuts to prepare fresh coconut milk, and Armand found some breadfruit to cook. Noelani, was amazed by the fresh fish, and the octopus still moving, changing colors. Mother Rota and Delphine's sister starting to prepare the meal. Meanwhile Delphine and Eiji were resting peacefully in their sleep. It was a day filled with happiness and satisfaction offering hope for renewal after the storm, for the entire family.

Chapter 8

Furusato

As the years go by, Joseph found himself taking on more responsibilities at the Hotel. An unexpected situation arose when Debra, the Sales and Marketing Manager who was due to attend the bi-annual Japan Travel Workshop could not go due to her pregnancy. She asked Joseph if he could go in her place and visit the travel agencies and be present at the Tahiti Workshops in Tokyo and Osaka. Hesitant at first, Joseph consulted with Monty the manager and Debra on their expectations and how to go about everything. Reassured, he arrived in Tokyo at Narita airport with the Tahiti delegation, hotel managers, sales directors and some staff of the local travel agencies. They boarded the Airport Limousine bus to the city, and Joseph realized how much Japan had changed since his childhood. It took an hour and a half to arrive in the capital, and the bus stopped at various hotels. The Tahiti delegation had rooms reserved at the Akasaka Tokyu, reviving memories of the house in Akasaka for the new salesman. Upon check-in Joseph is surprised by how tiny the rooms are in the city.

His former sempai, Ike from Safeway met him at the bar later in the evening. After some nostalgic reunion drinks, Ike invited him to talk a walk in the cool spring breeze outside the building. On the grand boulevard, the traffic was amazingly busy, and throngs of people were rushing into Akasaka subway station. The Sakura trees lining the boulevard had started to bloom. Reminiscing about his childhood, after a few blocks Joseph followed Ike into a side street and up a flight of concrete stairs, leading up to the entrance of another grand hotel, the Capitol Tokyu, the original Hilton hotel of Tokyo. As Joseph later learned, the hotel became the flagship of the Tokyu group. They took a flight of stairs down from the lobby to B1 to the Lipo Bar.

A three-piece Filipino live band was playing popular songs and a ravishing Filipina singer welcomed them by bowing. Joseph learns that Ike used to play at the same spot as professional drummer for a jazz band for many years before he made the move to Hawaii. His father who was Head of one of the biggest fresh produce wholesalers in Japan had asked Ike to study the produce business patterns in Hawaii and he regretted that he had to leave the music world. Ike was now practically running the company as his father would soon be retiring. A bottle of whisky appeared on the small table with a chain attached to its neck and Joseph could make out the letters in Japanese of Ike's last name. Wooden polished cabinets with glass doors stored valuable repeat customer's preferred drinks only to be taken out when the customer sat down. As Joseph settled into his comfortable chair, the bartender offered him a piping hot "oshibori"(pressed towel).

After drinks, Ike led him back upstairs through the lobby and they entered the Tempura restaurant. As they sat at the counter, Joseph witnessed how the chef gingerly dipped each item one by one into the special stainless-steel container of hot oil, and at the right moment scooped the vegetable with a small drainer utensil and placed this onto triple rectangular sheets of paper on the perfectly matching small plate. He found on the counter a tiny plate, with freshly grated daikon (white radish) to be stirred into the small bowl of dipping sauce. The daikon supposedly helped one digest the deep-fried vegetables, shrimp and fish. Joseph was delighted that meat was not an option in the tempura restaurant. The rectangular counter with the Chef in the middle only seated 6 persons at a time. A tempura'd vanilla ice cream dessert amazed Joseph.

They went back down to the Lipo Bar and the band was playing some samba jazz, doing a cover of "Corcovado". After ordering a second round, Ike whispered something to the barman. A few minutes later he came back with a room key and gave it to Joseph, saying that he was checked in as a guest of Ike, booked the rest of the week at the Capitol. He couldn't believe Ike's kind gesture. Joseph asked if he had any suggestions on how to get around town, as he hadn't taken the subway in so many years. Ike then surprised him again, that not to worry, he would have a car and chauffeur for him each day. Fatigued from jet lag and all the alcohol, Joseph thanked Ike and retired to his new room. Upon opening the door, he could not believe the size of the room which was so spacious. The window looked down at Hie Jinja, and he could see some of the Sakura in bloom, illuminated by the lamps above the Shinto temple.

Returning to his roots, his dreams were infused by images of his childhood. Whether it was a street or a familiar scenery, precious emotional moments resurfaced. In spite of the years gone by his heart was anchored to his "furusato" (native town) with authenticity weaving the past and the present together.

The Tahiti delegation had the weekend off to rest before the first workshop in Tokyo. On Sunday before noon, Ike came to pick up Joseph at the Capitol Tokyu having left his car in the hotel parking lot the night before. The comfortable Mercedes sedan passed by the Imperial Palace as Joseph marveled at the Sakura in bloom creating a magical pink flora covering the boulevards. As they reminisced about their days at Safeway, they arrived at a Sushi restaurant in the Nerima ward. Three Michelin stars adorned the entrance door.

Ike jokingly introduced Joseph to the master sushi chef, as an important friend who only spoke English. He bowed deeply offering "Haro my name izu Yoshinobu dozo irashaimase" welcome initiaing an animated and memorable encounter. For Joseph the exceptional quality of the sushi would be an unforgettable experience as he savored each nigiri with amazement. Joseph noticed the different sushi knives arranged on a shelf and the chef pointed out that the smallest one was originally three times its size. He learned that this was due to Yoshinobu's daily sharpening with special sharpening stones, altering the size after only two years. Fresh wasabi root was finely grated on traditional shark skin "oroshi"(vegetable grater). As Joseph tasted the tamago(egg roll) sushi, "Agari"(hot green tea) was served. The pungent aroma of the tea served at sushi counters made one relax after the meal. This "Kona-cha" or powder tea, is made from dust produced during the creation of green teas and blended with matcha.

Ike's hospitality extended to introducing his family to Joseph in their spacious home in the heart of Nerima. Senbei (rice crackers) and fresh strawberries appeared on a platter with Sencha tea, served by his graceful daughter, Akiko. Recalling their memories of Hawaii, they talked into the evening. Yumiko, his wife had prepared an exquisite Japanese dinner of grilled salmon, her homemade "tsukemono"(pickled vegetables), rice, miso soup, "chawanmushi"(steamed egg custard), and a salad of romaine lettuce with cherry tomatoes. It was a heartwarming reunion with his Sempai from Safeway.

Chapter 9

JR

Joseph's journey through the intricacies of the metro and JR (Japan Railways) system testified to his commitment to adapt to new environments and overcome obstacles with determination. Although the initial attempts might have been fraught with challenges, his perseverance eventually allowed him to master the intricacies of Tokyo's complex transportation system. His ability to seek help and utilize available resources demonstrated his willingness to learn and integrate into a new cultural environment. His dedication to successfully completing his mission, despite the challenges encountered along the way, spoke to his professionalism and commitment to the Hotel Bora Bora. At the Tokyo and Osaka workshops, Joseph's remarkable performance and ability to communicate in Japanese were praised by his colleagues and business partners, bolstering his reputation and opening new opportunities for the hotel in the Japanese market.

His transition from casual tropical attire to formal suits was certainly an adjustment for Joseph, but he quickly adapted to this new dress code. Awkwardly stepping away from Hawaiian Aloha shirts and lightweight pants, he soon recognized the importance of dressing appropriately for his professional role and for integrating into the Japanese business culture. Observing the dress standards of Japanese society, where luxury brands and tailored clothing were highly valued, Joseph proudly wore his ready-to-wear garments, reflecting his own authenticity and personal style. His adaptation to the new wardrobe was also symbolic of his ability to seamlessly integrate into diverse environments while maintaining his identity and self-confidence.

The journey on the Shinkansen (bullet train) was an impressive experience for Joseph, offering a unique combination of speed and comfort. As he moved through the changing landscapes of Japan, he savored a sushi bento, adding a touch of gastronomic pleasure to his trip. The speed of the train seemed almost surreal, swiftly passing urban buildings to reveal country side panoramas, providing a different perspective of the Japanese scenery. Immersed in a paperback book by Hemingway, Joseph found solace in the writer's words while traveling to his destination. Upon arrival at the Imperial Hotel in Osaka, he felt both amazed by modern technology and grateful for the opportunity to explore new horizons.

The dinner with Dr. Saeki and his wife Michiko was a memorable experience for Joseph, steeped in refinement and Japanese traditions. Set within the elegant surroundings of the sushi restaurant, the polished mahogany counter and the master sushi chef behind the chilled display case set the stage for an evening of culinary delights. Joseph was intrigued by Dr. Saeki's original drink, a mixture of Shochu over ice with sparkling water and a touch of fresh wasabi. Inspired by curiosity, he decided to follow suit and taste this unique beverage, while Michiko opted for a glass of white wine. Dr. Saeki's explanations about the benefits of fresh wasabi added to the drink were fascinating, offering new insights into Japanese culinary traditions and practices.

LUNCH AT THE HOTEL'S Teppanyaki restaurant was a delightful and entertaining experience for Joseph and his guests, travel agents from Osaka. Seated around the half-circle counter, they witnessed the chef's skill as he juggled ingredients and utensils while cooking on the hot grill in the center. The cuts of meat and seafood were prepared with impressive dexterity, and each bite was a true delight for the taste buds.

The guests were visibly surprised by Joseph's generosity in selecting this venue to thank them for their loyalty and contribution to the success of the Hotel Bora Bora. This friendly and memorable lunch strengthened the bonds between Joseph and the travel agents in Osaka, creating new opportunities to attract more visitors to Bora Bora.

Returning to Tokyo by Shinkansen, Joseph had a chance see Takashi and decided to meet in front of the Isetan Department Store in Shinjuku. They walked in an alleyway parallel to the boulevard and entered a traditional Sushi restaurant. Omakase (chef's suggestion or assortment of nigiri) was their choice as it was an inexpensive set menu and they toasted with glasses of cold Kirin beer. Behind the counter, Joseph sees an aquarium with a dozen aturés. He points out that he fishes these 'aji' or small jacks in Bora Bora. Upon hearing this, the Sushi chef scoops one out in a small net and prepares a dish in minutes. The fish is artistically arranged on a plate with green leaves and the fish presented on two small skewers imitating the fish in motion. The body area is carefully carved out with expertly cut slices of sashimi on the plate. As Joseph takes a piece with his chopsticks, the fish suddenly closes its mouth!

The liveliness of the aturé seems to defy the laws of nature, creating a surprising interaction between man and fish. The sushi master's creativity in presentation adds an artistic dimension to this culinary moment, making this tasting an unforgettable memory. It is a perfect illustration of the mastery and ingenuity that characterize Japanese cuisine, where every detail is carefully thought out to offer a unique sensory experience. In this warm atmosphere of conviviality, the two former colleagues renew their bond of friendship, both having become "saririman" or businessmen.

Chapter 10

Tokyo by Night

The unexpected evening in the bars of Akasaka and Ginza turned out to be a rewarding experience for Joseph, although initially planned as a simple business visit. After his presentation to the travel agents, he was pleasantly surprised by the invitation to dinner from the managing director. The visits to different bars in the area, the traditional Japanese restaurant, and finally the Celeste club in Ginza provided Joseph with an immersion into Tokyo's vibrant nightlife. Despite his fatigue, he was charmed by the warm atmosphere and hospitality of the hostesses and stayed late into the night grateful to his generous business partners.

The tasting of Fugu, a fish renowned for its toxicity, was a memorable experience for Joseph during his stroll in Shinjuku with Ike. Astonished by the delicacy of the paper thin slices of sashimi, Joseph learned the importance of having a qualified fugu master in every restaurant to serve this delicate dish safely. Accompanied by Ponzu (soy sauce seasoned with fresh citrus)and fresh chives and scallions, each morsel of Fugu was a delightful surprise. Joseph also had the opportunity to taste different parts of the fish, including the lightly grilled skin and the hirezake, a flambéed drink served with a piece of the fish's fin, offering extraordinary flavors. This unique culinary experience added an exotic note to his stay in Tokyo.

Immersed in an enchanting ambiance, Joseph discovers another aspect of Tokyo's music scene alongside Ike. In the intimate space of Club Doki Doki, a jazz band captivates the audience with classic tunes by Benny Goodman. Ike reveals that two of the band members have previously played together with him, evoking shared musical memories. With the sounds of the keyboard, clarinet, upright bass, guitar, saxophone, and drums, the cozy atmosphere of the club vibrates to the rhythm of jazz. Joseph marvels at how each musician contributes to creating a captivating experience, and he gets swept away by the infectious swing of the music, blending harmoniously into the enthusiastic crowd.

Joseph explores the culinary delights of Tokyo and discovers a new gastronomic gem, the Casita restaurant in Roppongi. Impeccable service and personalized attention transport him into an unforgettable evening, illuminated by delicate appetizers, champagne, and an exquisite dinner. Inspired by this experience, Joseph seeks a unique gift for Shigeru, owner of the restaurant as he was a loyal customer of Hotel Bora Bora and other resorts of the hotel group.

Between appointments in Shinbashi, Joseph enters The Japan Sword Company, where he finds a replica katana (sword) an iconic symbol of Japanese culture. He surprises Shigeru by presenting him with this exceptional gift. During this evening at Casita, Joseph dazzles the guests and the staff on the terrace of the restaurant, by performing a spectacular sabrage with Shigeru's katana, thus inaugurating an unexpected and festive tradition. The magic of this evening lingers in the annals of Casita restaurants in Tokyo, creating meaningful encounters and impressions.

Chapter 11

Worrisome Hearts

Seo-Yeon's news is both touching and imbued with courage. Despite the considerable challenges of her recovery, she displays remarkable resilience, supported by Hana's constant and loving presence. The transformation of her cane, from a simple walking aid to a symbol of her daily struggle, speaks volumes about her determination to overcome obstacles. Seo-Yeon's battle to regain her voice and memory is a true test, but every small progress is a victory to be celebrated. The comforting power of music, though initially difficult to endure, gradually becomes a catalyst for connection and memory. Through these trials, the friendship between Seo-Yeon and Hana shines as a beacon of support and hope. Their unwavering bond and Hana's unconditional love provide Seo-Yeon with clarity in darkness, illuminating her path to healing.

Hana's continued commitment to supporting Seo-Yeon in her recovery is admirable. She organized the devoted care of the speech therapist and physiotherapist reflecting hope and determination of the entire medical team to accompany Seo-Yeon on her journey. Every small progress, whether it's a facial expression or a regained bodily movement, is a source of encouragement and motivation for everyone looking after her. And the mere mention of Joseph's name being able to bring a smile to Seo-Yeon's face is proof of the significance of his friendship and support in this challenging recovery process. With the road ahead long and filled with obstacles, Hana's loving presence and the scheduled home visits by the medical staff offer hope for Seo-Yeon.

Joseph extends his deepest sympathy and support to Hana during this challenging time. He acknowledges the strength and determination she displays in caring for Seo-Yeon and offering her all the love and support possible. Sharing his own news, of professional responsibilities, travels, and family, demonstrates how much he values maintaining their friendship despite the distance between them. Expressing his desire to visit Seo-Yeon shows his commitment and genuine affection towards them both. In these difficult moments, simply knowing that he is there for them, even across the ocean, can bring some comfort and a sense of connection.

Chapter 12

Terima Kasih

The corporate marketing director's recognition and the trust she places in Joseph by entrusting him with broader responsibilities are clear signs of his effectiveness and professionalism. His ability to generate impressive mission reports during his trip to Japan was noticed and appreciated at a higher level within the organization. Being designated to represent Hotel Bora Bora at corporate meetings and subsequently invited for a six-week mission in Indonesia demonstrates that he has become a key player in the hotel group's marketing strategy. This opportunity to explore the group's other properties in Bali, Java, and the island of Moyo will not only allow him to deepen his knowledge of these destinations but also to contribute significantly to their promotion. This becomes an exciting evolution in his career that offers Joseph new perspectives and opportunities to showcase the unique attractions of each hotel within the group, while continuing to successfully represent the exclusivity and charm of Hotel Bora Bora.

In these magnificent hotels, every detail seems to have been carefully thought out to offer a luxurious and serene experience to every guest. Joseph is amazed by the size and beauty of the villas, as well as their clean interiors that highlight natural light and teak wood elements. The atmosphere exudes tranquility and voluptuousness, reminiscent of Baudelaire's enchanting verses. Every interaction with the staff is filled with respect and courtesy, symbolized by warm greetings like "Selamat Pagi" (good morning) as they bow their heads placing their hands together. Joseph quickly finds himself immersed in this culture of hospitality and reciprocates the gestures of respect. The day begins with sumptuous breakfasts and unfolds in a setting of absolute tranquility and comfort. The experience evokes a sense of calm and well-being, allowing Joseph to fully recharge and relax.

The discovery of the village of Tenganan was a fascinating experience for Joseph, offering him an authentic glimpse into Balinese tradition. Located on the east coast of Bali, this ancestral village exudes a timeless atmosphere, as if time had stopped centuries ago. Exploring the ancient rocky road lined with house entrances and symbolic levels, Joseph was able to grasp the importance of social hierarchy within the community. The villagers' decision to open their doors to visitors only recently, allowed Joseph to admire and acquire some unique works of art, showcasing Bali's ancestral craftsmanship. From wooden sculptures to hand-woven fabrics to miniature paintings on bamboo, each creation tells a story and carries deep meaning in the local culture. During his visit, Joseph felt like he saw his daughter Noelani in the face of one of the village girls, an experience that seemed almost magical. This encounter with the beauty and authenticity of Tenganan undoubtedly marked his journey to Bali, offering him a precious insight into the island's cultural richness.

The majesty of the Pacific Ocean, reminiscent of the waves of Tahiti, stretched out before Joseph as he gazed from the hotel built on a cliff. This establishment was a true architectural marvel, with its three stacked infinity pools descending towards the lookout point, offering breathtaking views. Although Joseph hesitated to swim among the other guests, his early departure the next day presented him with an unexpected opportunity. In the dim light of early morning, Joseph decides to venture into the pool. As he pauses to savor the tranquility and splendor of the moment, a hotel staff member, dressed in white, offers him a large towel and greets him with a respectful "Bapak Joseph Selamat Pagi"(Sir Joseph, Good morning). Joseph is amazed to receive such service even in the early hours of dawn, a testament to the exceptional commitment of the staff to the comfort and well-being of the guests.

On the island of Moyo, the architect had endeavored to preserve the natural environment and essence of the jungle by creating expansive double-canvas tents, resembling individual villas, topped by a unique roofing. The property extended along a beautiful beach, reminiscent to Joseph of the entire shoreline of Matira in Bora Bora, devoid of constructions at the water's edge. Inside the tent, the space was vast yet simply decorated, with a large four poster bed reigning at the center, draped with a mosquito net. Guests were given the choice to enjoy air conditioning or opt for the rustic ceiling fan suspended above. The only sounds Joseph heard were those of birds and monkeys in the surrounding trees, offering a natural serenade to his temporary retreat.

As he made his way to the shore, attentive staff offered him mask, snorkel, and fins and Joseph plunged into the lagoon to discover a fascinating underwater spectacle. Hundreds of small trevally circled beneath the pontoon, and a myriad of tropical fish in every corner graced the crystal-clear waters. Upon his return, the staff had been informed of his interest in fishing, and he was invited on a trolling fishing excursion, where he had the pleasure of catching several bluefin trevally, adding an adventurous touch to his paradise stay.

In Java, Joseph discovers the limestone villas in Yogyakarta, near the famous Buddhist temple, Borobudur. The hotel takes inspiration from the temple, paying homage to its circular spaces and levels. An atmosphere steeped in religion permeates every corner, with a majestic silence only broken by the chirping of birds and the Muslim call to prayer.

Awakened before dawn, Joseph embarks on his journey to the temple, accompanied by a driver in total darkness. In the obscure early morning, he explores the mysteries of the temple with an Indonesian guide, a French speaker with a Parisian accent. Together, they climb the levels, marveling at the bas-reliefs carved in stone, recounting the story of Buddha's life. At the summit, they contemplate the first rays of sunlight, bathing the stupas and bodhisattvas in an orange glow, offering a breathtaking view of the sunrise from this ancient edifice dating back to the 8th century.

Back in Bali, at Denpasar airport, Joseph is greeted by his driver dressed in immaculate white attire, ready to take him back to his temporary residence in Ubud. As they leave the bustling main roads filled with scooters and motorcycles, the landscape transforms, giving way to lush greenery where vast rice paddies stretch, adorning the plains and valleys with their vibrant green glow. Navigating the winding paths, Joseph marvels at villagers offering flower and incense on altars in front of their homes, as well as on the roads, ensuring goodwill for travelers. Silence reigns supreme on this mythical island, where the deafening noises of machines are replaced by the gentle murmur of rivers and the chirping of birds. Tasks are carried out with meticulousness and respect: grass is manicured with scissors, and trenches are dug with picks, all in a commitment to environmental preservation. Joseph is deeply moved by this harmony between man and nature, where authenticity and mutual respect prevail. He expressed his gratitude to the humble Balinese staff by bowing, placing his hands together and pronouncing the words "terima kasih" (thank you).

Chapter 13

Touristic

Joseph's return to Bora Bora is marked by the joy of reuniting with his family, but also by the realization of the changes on the island. Indeed, he discovers that Delphine has started working at a new hotel, an exciting venture for her but also indicative of the growing development in the island's hotel sector. The surge in tourism is also reflected in the increasing population and number of vehicles, gradually transforming the image of the island. However, despite these changes, Joseph feels a certain longing for the silence and authenticity he found in Bali, thus realizing the cultural differences between the two destinations. Nevertheless, reuniting with his family in this tropical paradise remains a moment of happiness and comfort for him.

Joseph adeptly balances his new marketing responsibilities with his commitments within the hotel. He is called upon to organize VIP events, cocktail parties, and warmly welcome Japanese guests, as well as promoting the hotel through articles in local media. Weddings held at the Bora Bora Town Hall have become a marketing opportunity, and Joseph takes charge of documenting these special moments with newspaper articles and photos, showcasing the hotel's idyllic setting.

Despite his busy schedule, Joseph always finds time to enjoy the simple pleasures of life on the island. Waiting for Delphine in the evening, he gazes out at the lagoon and relaxes by fishing, bringing home a harvest of aturés and trevally. This was the perfect way to end the day, in harmony with nature and appreciating the tranquility of this paradise environment.

The reduction in the number of bungalows at Hotel Bora Bora, inspired by resorts from the group in Indonesia and Thailand, aims to offer a more exclusive and personalized service to the guests. The new villas, located on the beach or in the gardens, some with their own private pool, are designed to provide a high level of comfort and privacy. The introduction of telephones in each room marks a significant evolution, although some accustomed guests prefer to set aside this modernity to fully appreciate the tranquility and simplicity of their stay. These changes demonstrate the hotel's commitment to adapting to the needs and preferences of its clientele while preserving the essence of the authentic Bora Bora experience.

Chapter 14

Waiting for you

Joseph's upcoming trip to Japan, including a stay in South Korea, promises to be a rewarding experience both professionally and personally. The prospect of exploring this new Korean market, which is constantly evolving according to the group's hotel reports, fills him with excitement. The contact with Hana and the prospect of reuniting with Seo-Yeon added a warm dimension to this journey. The preparations, including the carefully selected Polynesian gifts by Delphine, reflect Joseph's attention and consideration towards his Korean hosts. Despite some anxiety, this long-awaited meeting promises to be filled with precious moments and unforgettable memories.

The pleasant flight experience with the upgrade to Business Class was certainly a great start to this journey. Joseph's decision to take the Narita Express to save time in Tokyo demonstrates his efficiency and determination to optimize his schedule. Upon arriving at the Capitol Tokyu Hotel, he is greeted by a letter from Hana, adding a personal touch to his already promising stay.

The news of the tragedy that befell Hana and Seo-Yeon is heartbreaking. Joseph is overwhelmed by shock and pain as he reads the letter. The sudden loss of Seo-Yeon leaves an immense void, and words seem inadequate to express the sorrow he feels. He cannot contain his grief, and his cries of despair resonate in the hotel room. Despite the distance, the pain is as poignant as if he were present.

Hana had been courageous, staying by Seo-Yeon's side until the end. The weeks leading up to this moment have been filled with sadness and mourning, and Mi-Cha and Steven made the journey from New York to be at the funeral. Joseph's arrival was a ray of hope in the darkness, where everything seemed bleak and insurmountable. Despite the pain, Hana will be at Incheon Airport, ready to welcome Joseph, even in her own grief.

Notwithstanding such agony weighing heavily on her, Hana remains dignified and composed. Clad in black, she bears the marks of her grief with silent grace. Joseph greets her respectfully, acknowledging the strength she must summon to be there despite everything. Her features are marked by sorrow, but her regal like bearing and elegant demeanor reveal remarkable resilience. Even in her despair, she displays remarkable courtesy and attention towards Joseph. The BMW car contrasts with the emotionally charged atmosphere, but it also reflects Hana's determination to maintain some semblance of normalcy in this ordeal.

Hana drives Joseph to the cemetery, and on the way, Joseph had asked to stop at a florist to pick up flowers. These small gestures from her friend, whom she meets for the first time after years of correspondence, elicit a smile. Kneeling before Seo-Yeon's grave, Joseph offers his prayer, shedding tears that touch Hana, and she finds her own tears of anguish.

Continuing their drive, she stops the car at the foot of the mountain in Namsan Park to offer Joseph a cable car ride and enjoy the observation tower. Joseph discovers a panoramic view of the city, and he sees on the horizon the Pacific Ocean. Hana remembered the sisters talking about their tour of Oahu with Joseph. She invites him to a restaurant near the park, and Joseph tries authentic Korean kimchi and a delicious seafood bibimbap.

Joseph is pleasantly surprised to be upgraded to a VIP suite at the hotel. He understands that Hana, having stayed in luxury hotels before with Seo-Yeon, was given some privileges. She accompanies Joseph to check the suite, and Joseph wanted to present her with the gifts. He had found the perfect gift in Narita, a yellow metal box adorned with a drawing of a dove, containing Hato Saburé biscuits. It was a symbol of his love for Seo-Yeon and his newfound connection with Hana. She also appreciated the small Tahitian gifts. In the large living room of the suite, Hana hugs Joseph and begins to sob. In the Terrace restaurant of the Grand Hyatt, they enjoy a buffet dinner together in honor of their dear departed love.

Hana's presence and collaboration became fundamental for Joseph during his stay in Seoul. As an interpreter, guide and driver, she facilitated communication in a different linguistic environment, allowing Joseph to forge meaningful connections with Korean travel agents. Thanks to this partnership, Joseph achieved his business goals and planned to return regularly to Korea to further develop this market.

Chapter 15

A time for all

Joseph's return to Bora Bora provides him with both a glimpse of progress and transformation on the island, but also a sense of inner emptiness, like Urashima Taro returning to a deserted beach. Despite the tourist development and the benefits it brings to the local population, Joseph feels nostalgic for a bygone era, when the island may have been more authentic and preserved. As he cycles around the island, he contemplates the familiar landscape from Hamaire hill. He finds solace in the timeless beauty of the turquoise lagoon and Mount Otemanu. Closing his eyes and letting himself be carried away by memories and images of distant friends, he is like a cat resting in a hinata bocco pose.

The sight of a few strands of white hair in the reflection of a car window serves as a tangible reminder of the passage of time, but also as a symbol of maturity and acquired experience. For Joseph, these white strands are not just a sign of age, but perhaps a hint of wisdom. As he continues his journey on his bicycle, he reflects on his unique path, acknowledging the highs and lows, the joys and challenges that have shaped his journey thus far. It is in this acceptance of oneself and one's history that Joseph finds a deep inner peace, allowing him to fully appreciate the present and embrace the future with serenity, in an island paradise.

About the Author

David Nakano lives in French Polynesia. He enjoys riding his bicycle on the island roads and is a volunteer as manager of a local cycling club, Vélo Club Bora Bora.